MEDWIN'S ROOM
TERMINA ASHTON

MEDWIN'S ROOM

TERMINA ASHTON

MEDWIN'S ROOM

Termina Ashton

For my children,
life is fantastic because you are part of mine

Medwin's Room

Chapter 1

THE CURIOUS DWELLER

It was a breezy morning, one where most would prefer to stay in comfort by the warmth of an open fire and not unlike most other days, as the trees formed a blanket of protective cover across much of the landscape, keeping the region quite cool, almost impenetrable. On occasion the sun's rays would filter through cracks of foliage, warming parts of these mountains east of Victoria, aiding the growth of the forest, hence the tall gums and carpet clusters of shrubs.

Medwin Rune tossed the woolen wrap across his shoulders then rubbed his palms causing the friction to warm his iced hands. Reaching for his head, he straightened the spiral turban, which today was a vibrant orange; this colour complimented his loose-fitting pants and the flowing silk fabrics he wrapped around his torso.

After a slight stretch and a drawn in scent of the eucalyptus, Medwin began his trek through the well-used path of overgrowth and crushed leaves, passing through these natural obstacles with a swoop of his jagged cane. The cane was adorned with a coil of geometric carvings and he always carried it with him upon his daily visits to the local village. Perhaps it was simply a handy device to keep his balance, after all, the ground was not very level.

The surrounding sounds were tranquil with the exception for a family of cockatoos that rustled through a wild bush of blackberries to cater for their daily breakfast. *1949, yet another year*, he thought as he watched the birds maneuver through the thorns to pluck the berries.

"My, how time has a way of escaping," whispered Medwin to himself and stopped as he fumbled for a moment searching his thoughts for his age. "One seems to lose count when the grid of wrinkles appear. Needless to say, it has no importance. I still feel sixty years younger, possibly more," he croaked a soft chuckle and continued his steady pace to the village.

The locals were quite neighbourly and formed a friendly community amongst themselves; however, all found Medwin quite peculiar, mostly because of his uncommon ways and unconventional dress sense, particularly the colours,

"oh come on," some of the men would say, "what kind of a bloke wears bright pink?"

Medwin possessed no vehicle. He walked everywhere with ease holding that stick that was more like a pole the villagers would say. "Pretty fit for an old fella", was another favourite, and "I reckon that pole must weigh a tonne".

Regardless of Medwin's eccentricities, all the town folk liked him very much. He was somewhat of an icon. Rune the Recluse they nicknamed him.

It was unknown how long Medwin had been part of this town. The locals could only gather, other than his profession and old age, that this man preferred the company of his pet possum, mostly. It was quite humorous to see him walk alongside the marsupial everywhere he went.

Though he did not speak often, Medwin would always nod his greeting with a gentle smile. On the few occasions when he spoke, his voice was quiet with a shaky British accent, not at all like the Aussie tones that was predominant in town.

Medwin lived very much as a hermit and never bought groceries or any conveniences from the local stores. He would graciously refuse and thank any offers, once adding that he grew his own produce. Any other living elements were a mystery to the residents.

The other known fact across the region was the abilities this man possessed to heal and foresee the future. It was upon his daily treks that Medwin offered his services at no expense to anybody in need. He would perform these tasks with softly spoken chants and the crowds would eagerly gather, listening to his distorted whispers, always attempting to make sense of the sounds. This also triggered curiosity amongst the locals, providing hot gossip and stories they shared with each other and visitors, often adding more colour to the truth.

The bond between Medwin and his pet was apparent, and they did everything together, including the healing rituals; the well-trained possum always aided Medwin by rattling a chesty chant.

Watching this really was an unusual sight and never was it carried out privately. Medwin always sat his customer upon a public chair surrounded by fascinated, sometimes skeptical onlookers. Then he would encircle his patient as the possum followed his lead.

The town children enjoyed watching the furry friend take part and eagerly waited for a chance to pat the marsupial once the healing process was complete. The possum seemed to enjoy the affection as did Medwin, who would stand in the background watching the crowd through soft, fluid green eyes and stretching a gentle smile.

This curious old man resided upon one of the elevated blocks along the main street, his immense house surrounded by many acres of lush vegetation.
The gardens were breathtaking, containing full blooms of flowers and shrubs with tall conifers forming a fort wall, encasing everything within the property. Medwin had pruned gaps of symmetrical shapes, within these natural walls, allowing the locals only a glimpse of what lay beyond.

Two large solid gates of black iron was the only entry point to the estate. Both gates were layered with stringed iron vines, climbing up the face and meeting at the top to encase a triangular sign, carved from stone. The locals assumed that this sign once contained the name of the estate, but for unknown reasons it had been deliberately etched out leaving no writing, except for scrapes on the surface.

Medwin's home was quite a large house for one man and his pet, certainly different from the other neighbouring homes. Constructed of timber with an array of shapes, it resembled a bunch of building blocks placed together. This oblong house had a hexagon attached to each side and was sealed with a flat diamond roof. Upon the roof for a third story, a coned bell tower sat centered, holding a hollow square frame swaying at its tip.

Inside, a wide stairwell led to all the living areas on the second level. The enormous fireplace in the lounge room, made entirely of black rocks, dominated the first view atop of the landing. Twelve-foot ceilings towered over the immense spaces, with the exception of some areas that had suspended ceilings, edged with steps and were held afloat with tension rods.

Upon the centre of all ceilings in each room, a painted feature in the shape of a black diamond rested. This diamond matched those on the whitewashed timber floors. The dining area only, displayed a prominent tiled slab, rough and chunky like badly carved stone, the only grey flooring in the house surrounded by the same-whitewashed surface. Once again, symmetrical shapes as hollow niches in the white walls acted as windows, contrasting rooms concealed with black doors. Medwin had etched white numbers upon each door, including the entry point; perhaps this helped to jog his memory due to ageing.

This home was not the standard type of dwelling in these parts, not even for this time, but Medwin Rune was not your standard type of person for this time or, quite frankly, any other.

Unbeknownst to the locals, Medwin was, in truth, the Summit Oracle, the only of his kind and, most importantly, he was the bearer and protector of all hidden secrets and mysteries.

The certainty of other dimensions was one of these secrets, containing worlds where beings and creatures exist just as humans do, only in different surroundings. Medwin possessed the knowledge to open these gateways and the ability to enter through to these wondrous worlds, hidden from most, including the human beings.

For many years, Medwin carried out daily incantations and had trekked about all worlds discovering the identities of each creator, and it was in one of these worlds where he met his inseparable furry companion.

Foremost, he learned that these gateways were not in fact as they appeared, but were forms of illusion, manifested through a secret held by each creator and, should one obtain the knowledge, these worlds were fragile to change. Granted this knowledge, only Medwin held the ultimate key to all dimensions.

Respected by all who knew his true self, but envied by those wishing for power, Medwin unfortunately crossed paths with two beings, neither of whom had any powers in the human dimension but were able to control and manipulate the worlds of the gateways for their own purposes through deceit, magic, and cold power.

These beings learned of the responsibility Medwin privately protected and, desperately wanting to uncover the most crucial secrets by any means they began a private war, disposing of each creator in order to weaken any combined efforts Medwin might gain through their power. In addition, they seized the inhabitants and forced them to reveal the whereabouts of the Oracle.

Medwin became concerned upon this discovery, and fear gripped all his senses, when he detected that the two beings were in search of five items he held in trust.

These five items were the path to reach the all-important key and were indestructible; it was this key that held importance for all life forms. If the two power-driven beings obtained knowledge of the sacred secrets, they would gain powers to control and manipulate all worlds, including the human world.

Worst of all, they would conquer and rule without any chance of reversal.

This knowledge forced Medwin's decision to hide in the human world. His loyal possum friend followed. Hidden deep in the mountains, Medwin became a local and nobody knew of his real powers. As for the crucial items, Medwin veiled all five of them, cautiously adding incantations and bewitched a trail towards the key.

Though the two beings had minimal power, deceit can be a strong motivator; they searched for Medwin over many years. It was the year of 1949 on that breezy day, not unlike any other, when Medwin's world collapsed.

The beings had finally discovered his whereabouts. Unable to use magic, they worked their ability to trick and deceive the Oracle into entering a gateway. The gateway to a world they had conquered and now control.

Medwin very soon realised he had been enticed into a trap, giving the beings a chance to escape through the entry to search for and—worse—steal the items. With rapid speed, the protector performed an incantation sealing the gateway, imprisoning all within; in addition, he bewitched a path to his location.

Dread began to fill his emotions, and with many of his secrets left behind, he hoped these would never get into the wrong hands.

Chapter 2

THE COAXING FORCE

"Are we there yet?"

"Soon, alright! Stop asking or at least use a different sentence," Therese said and rolled her eyes. Now Jade had Micky saying it too. She picked up the poster-sized chart and scanned their location. "According to this map, we go under a bridge and then it's not far from there."

Therese and her kids were becoming anxious yet were still very excited. It had been a tough year with the divorce and all, so a holiday in the mountains was just the perfect way to forget all their worries and work out new plans for the next year, the big 2000. They had just passed the bridge when they spotted a sign welcoming them to Yarra Glen.

"Wow, this place is so nice," Jade noted the lush green surroundings and wound down her window to smell the scent of gum trees. Therese nodded and continued her struggle to read the awkward sized map. It was a beautiful place.

"The motel is only about 4km up the road judging by the distance chart on this map, so it's definitely not long now. Whoo hoo! I can't wait to vege out." Therese cheered, and her children joined in.

They had been traveling for hours and finally their destination was close. Suddenly, there was a clunk and their silver station wagon came to a stop.

"What! Damn it!" Therese complained. "This is a Holden. This can't happen, damn it!"

"Mum!" exclaimed Jade. "Micky can hear you."

"I know I'm sorry, block your ears. It's just really annoying. I had the car serviced before we left. What's the problem? Damn mechanics. I bet he knows my ex," Therese grumbled further.

"Muuummm!" Jade exclaimed again and placed both palms over her brother's ears.

"I know. I know. Micky can hear."
Therese got out of the car, kicked the door shut, and had a quick look, but she could not find anything wrong. *I'll call road service*, she thought then reached into the car to grab her mobile phone and knocked her head on the doorframe when she heard Micky squeal.

"Hi kitty," he giggled and waved at the same time.

"What kitty?" Therese looked about. But she could not see anything, only trees. Shrugging, she continued for the phone, picked it up and dialed...Nothing. "What now!" she growled. "Great! There's no service. This is so annoying too, I don't even know where a phone box is." Tapping her fingernails on the phone, she searched her thoughts for a moment. "I know! I'll go knock on someone's door. Hopefully I can use their phone."

Therese scanned the area, but all she could see was the tip of a roof surrounded by overgrown plantation. Grabbing her purse, she turned to the children, her brow creased in concern.

"You two stay in the car. Lock the doors and, Jade, keep an eye on Micky, please. I'm going to this house okay. I'll be as quick as I can."
With a deep breath and a few irate mumbles, she began her walk toward the old house, turning when she heard Jade call out.

"We want to come too."

Holding back a smile, Therese grunted. "Okay you two monkeys but behave."
They began the trek up the steep driveway edged with a row of purple and white agapanthus in full bloom, getting denser as they neared the entrance to the property. Therese could feel butterflies building in her stomach when only a few steps stood between them and the large gates that were slightly ajar. The tall structures had weathered so much over time that they were quite stiff to push open. Still with a good nudge and forced body weight, Therese managed to open the gates further, the creaking just added to the eerie sense she felt about entering this property.

Jade and Micky did not seem disturbed at all; Micky giggled as he ran ahead, almost tripping with excitement, whilst Jade stopped to study the sign above the gates. The weathered plaque was blank but showed visible signs of vandalism.

"Hmm," Jade said to herself mostly, "I wonder what was written on it."

Twelve year old, Jade Jarrod, a curious child with wide hazel eyes always alert, absorbed her surroundings like a sponge. Quite the little academic for her age, some would call her a genius, but she would justify her knowledge, modestly saying it was just common sense and refused to speak in words that made her stand out from the rest. Jade loved a mystery. Her goal in life was to become an archaeologist and she would often study her fascination of past worlds, passionately believing she would be the one who discovered Atlantis.

A quick-witted tomboy and average in height, Jade never wore a dress or anything to highlight her pretty features and petite frame. Her long, mouse brown hair cascaded down to her hips and was the envy of many girls, yet she most often wore it in a disheveled ponytail.

Therese could never understand why a tomboy would want to have such long hair. After all, she too had been a tomboy at the same age, but her hair was kept at shoulder length and Jade was the image of herself. Therese would often get annoyed with Jade because she avoided the hairbrush as much as possible. Therese called it spaghetti hair and was always on Jade's case about looking after it. "You're so pretty," she would say, "put something nice on and brush that bird's nest."

But Jade loved the weathered look and believed it complimented her well-loved camouflage or 'camo' clothes, that she always wore, much to her mother's dismay. Regardless, Therese adored her girl and was always the proud parent.

Like her daughter in many ways, Therese also had a lust for learning and commitment to see things through, though her interests leaned more toward arts and crafts. She did not possess the genius qualities of Jade, but her intellect was quite worldly, yet still somewhat naïve. She could find positive outcomes in all experiences even though she seemed sarcastic along the way and sometimes 'airy fairy,' as Jade would say. Her lust for life was apparent, and she aimed to find fun in all her ventures, but sometimes her concern could toss a spanner in the works, more so because of her overprotective nature with her children.

Jade turned, her thoughts still pondering on the sign and she followed her mother up the driveway, her steps moving quicker to catch up, because Therese broke into a jog to catch an escaping toddler. Jade laughed, she could see Micky giggling and squirm as her mother picked him up then maneuvered him around her waist to piggy back him up to the house. He was always full of beans.

Michael Jarrod, nicknamed Micky, was an active two-year-old, who possessed an attitude of no fear, and he did everything like a greyhound in a race; his favorite hobbies included everything he could attempt or touch. He began to communicate quite early, from the age of one, and spoke with a lisp, using his own version of words, missing letters and sometimes adding a few on occasion.

Micky too was the image of his mother, except for his eyes, which were bright green with long dark lashes. His soft straight hair was cropped short and never seemed to tangle or kink. Jades favourite tease was 'Mushroom head,' she called him this because of the bowl style cut, but it suited his round face, particularly the way his cheeks puffed when he smiled, which was quite often.

The trio reached the bend at the top of the driveway and could now see the house in full view. Breathing in the overriding scent of ginger lilies, they pushed through the overgrown weeds and ivy along the path, revealing pockets of bright yellow daffodils. The pebbled driveway was lined with rosebushes, each budding roses in different colours, it widened at the foot of the house, ending at the parking bay, centered with a concrete fountain in the shape of a large diamond.

This garden would have been stunning, at one time, Therese thought, surprised to see the flowers in such perfect growth, especially with the obvious years of neglect. She turned her focus toward the house and gasped in awe along with Jade, as they surveyed the dwelling. They felt drawn to this house. It too had been neglected but, surprisingly, the exterior did not appear to need much repair. In fact, a closer inspection revealed that it was simply covered in a lot of dust and cobwebs.

"Wow!" exclaimed Jade, "It's huge!" Therese agreed, and both stood silent for a moment, as they absorbed more of the surroundings, particularly the mass of the house. Everything on the exterior was a crisp white, except the roof.

A black roof. Who has a black roof? Therese wondered.

"Kitty! Kitty! Kitty!" Micky broke the silence with his squeaky voice and began giggling, as he blew kisses and waved his other hand frantically.

Therese and Jade spun around but once again could not see a cat. They looked around again, still nothing. Suddenly, Jade threw her arm forward and pointed as she bellowed,
"there it is, over there! But..." she thought a moment, "it's a brush-tail possum."
They all studied the plump grey creature, perched on the portico handrail, the rattle of its chest loud. It was the size of a large domestic cat.

"That's really weird, mum," whispered Jade. "I looked there a second ago and it wasn't there! Doo roon doo roon doo roon," she began to chant her version of a spooky tune.

"Enough, shoosh," snapped Therese.
Jade smiled and stopped the chant. Therese could see that her daughter was not afraid at all. In fact, she had the look of excitement in her eye and eagerly awaited the steps forward to an adventure she was hoping for.

"Oh, it's gorgeous," Therese said and walked closer to the possum, Jade followed close behind. "It's well fed, too."

The rattling sound stopped, and the eerie feeling returned as the possum ogled them, looking back and forth, only moving its eyes, still perched on the rail. Both Therese and Jade froze where they stood, unable to speak. Micky simply continued giggling and was tapping on his mother's head, using it like a bongo drum singing boom, boom, boom.
The eerie feeling vanished and now a warm sense of welcome washed through them. The frozen stance lasted only a few seconds, and the possum moved, curling itself into a ball to begin a nap.

"Should we knock?" Jade asked, popping with excitement.

"We don't have to," Therese replied, rather casually, as she carefully slid Micky down from his piggyback. His feet zoomed off, barely touching the ground towards the possum, giggling with his arms outstretched; he adored animals and could not wait to hug the fur ball. "Micky, no," she hollered but it was too late, he was already patting the possum.

"Why not?" Jade asked in a puzzled tone.

"Because there's no one here, except for that fat possum. Come on," she prompted her daughter to walk forward.

Puzzled even more, Jade stared at her mother and she scratched her head, trying to find the answer. Therese rushed for Micky, pulling him away from the possum. After all, it was a wild creature and she was afraid it would hurt her baby boy with its sharp claws. Jade continued her perplexed look. *Mum's acting weird*, she thought, but this did not surprise her too much; her mother and her creative ways would often go off on a tangent, and she would always explain her brainstorm during its process.

But, far from weird was Therese's state of mind. There was a connection, she could feel it. Never had her instincts been so conclusive. She curved her arm around Jade's shoulder giving her a caressing squeeze and guided her towards the front steps of the entry point.

"Ready kids. Let's have a look at our new home," she smiled at Jade's confused expression.

"What!" Jade was stunned but equally excited; like her mother, she felt this wonderful force draw her toward the home.
They began to ascend the semi-circle stairs. Therese, still holding Micky, gently moved her free arm down and took hold of Jade's hand. Micky stretched and managed to grasp the possum, then dished out a session of kisses and squeezes to the much appreciative fur ball.

"Micky," snapped Therese in concern but he refused to break his embrace.

This possum was unusually tame. Not wanting to interrupt the warm greeting the two enjoyed Therese exhaled a sigh of relief assured that the possum would not hurt her son and they all continued forward.

Standing at the front door, with the handle in reach, once again Therese felt the butterflies. *I'll turn the handle and hope for the best.* She let go of Jade's hand, then winked, forcing a smile, she shrugged her shoulders at the same time, in an attempt to show excitement, rather than show Jade that she was nervous. She reached for the knob, but it did not turn; instead the door pivoted open with ease. The panel was quite wide and thick with no hinges; it simply contained a central rod enabling the door to spin.

Fit new lock, Therese made a mental note in her mind, starting her 'to do' list.

Taking hold of Jade's hand once again, Therese led her family and Micky's new play pet into the house.

Chapter 3

HOME IS WHERE THE FATE IS

Therese and Jade stood in the entry foyer staring at the freestanding staircase leading to the upper level. The base was at least six metres wide, and narrowed, as it ascended in a curved swoop. There were no internal walls only two huge hexagon rooms on either side of the stairwell. The entire space was completely white except for the curtains, front door, and the etched diamond shape, centered on the floor of each room, which were all black. There was no furniture, only a canvas painting suspended from the centre ceiling of each room, floating only about two inches off the floor. These paintings also were white, with a black diamond shape, painted in the centre.

Micky began to jiggle and squirm out of his mother's grip. Therese slid him down, laughing as she watched him squeal with excitement. He was free to run wild amidst this vast open space and still he managed to hold the plump possum in his embrace. He shot off to swing on the artwork.

Therese scanned the rooms for a light switch. *That's odd*, she thought, *there aren't any*? She looked on all the walls and framework, Jade aided in the search, but nothing.

"There aren't even any power points, mum," Jade darted across the rooms still searching.

Therese looked up and realised there was not a single light fitting either, not even any exposed wiring to show there might have been something previously. "Oh well mental note. 'To do,' need electrical fittings," she muttered to herself.

"Let's go upstairs, Mum, come on..." urged Jade, "I can't wait to see how big it is." Therese was quick to respond; her curiosity was tempted as well.

"Come on, Micky," she called, "let's go up." Micky let go of the artwork, giving it a good swing before he shot off, running towards the stairs. The possum had already begun the climb up the staircase, after Micky had let go, realising it was easier to use two hands to swing on the artwork, like a jungle vine. The possum stopped a few times, looking back, as if waiting for the family to catch up. They all ascended the stairs with Micky taking the lead, crawling upon his hands and knees, copying his play pet.

Now standing upon the top landing, Therese and Jade stopped to observe the scene before them, once again they were in awe.

"Wow!" they both exclaimed, "this house is fantastic!" Just standing in one spot revealed so much of the interior.

It had curved walls, half walls, high ceilings, lower ceilings and open niches in most walls. A huge fireplace taller than Therese, spread across the lounge room wall. The kitchen dominated by a galley bench had a potbelly stove positioned against a wall. There were doors with glass knobs, enclosing some rooms and a spiral staircase leading up to a bell tower. Again, they viewed more of the canvas paintings centered in most rooms and the house was furnished, too.

They ran around opening doors, finding bedrooms and bathrooms with concrete baths. In the kitchen, there was a double door that opened to what seemed to be a walk-in pantry but housed a concrete washtub, Therese assumed it was the laundry. This house was a smorgasbord of shapes, yet with all this great design there was no colour, only black, grey and white throughout the house.

"I love it," cheered Therese. "We could do so much with this place. A bit of renovating and splashes of colour, will make it more amazing." Her ideas were running at rapid speeds.

"I can't wait, mum. This house is unreal." Jade stopped suddenly, then looked toward her mother and asked with a concerned voice, "But, what if it's not for sale."

Therese smiled. "Oh, honey girl, come here," and Jade walked over to the warm embrace of her mother. "It is for sale. There's a Realtor board near the front gate, hidden in the bushes. See? I'm not that crazy," she finished with a laugh.

"Cool bananas," Jade bellowed. They both jumped and danced around with excitement. "Come on, come on, come on, let's go and buy it," she begged.

Micky was also squealing with excitement. Not so much at the prospect of buying the house, but because he was having an absolute ball running about the house, making train sounds whilst the possum followed, like a passenger in the rear cabin. Therese took hold of Micky's hand and they all exited the house laughing as they brainstormed ideas of things they could do with the house, when reality struck. They were so caught up in this fantasy, they had forgotten the initial reason for entering the property.

"The car," Therese interrupted, "I still need to find a phone," thinking for a moment she suggested they return to the vehicle, check the map and see how far the local village was. They could probably walk there and get some help.

They all hopped into the motionless station wagon. Therese checked her phone, hoping there would be some little miracle.

"That's weird," she muttered, and she was puzzled. "I've got reception now, hmm, that's better. I wonder if the car will start too. Another miracle would be great."

The car revved on the first turn. *Hmm*, not wanting to question their luck, she was just thankful that it started. She placed it into gear and began to drive, once again heading for the motel.

"Are we going to the realtor, mum?" Jade eagerly waited for the response.

"I think we should go to the motel and check in first," even though she was equally as excited as her daughter was.

"But..." Jade complained, her plea cut short.

"But nothing, honey girl," Therese ended the petition suggesting they get settled first and then they can find out about the house.

Jade puckered out her bottom lip in disappointment but knew it was the best thing to do at first, and even though she would never admit it, she loved her nickname, 'honey girl'; it always made her smile and feel good. But this time it did not curb her frustration; she was just so excited, it was making her impatient.

They arrived at the motel and checked in. Therese was unloading the suitcases when Jade smiled broadly.

"I saw the realtor office, mum. It's across the road over there, see," she pointed at the direction and read, "Bob Upwey Real Estate."
It was a stroke of luck, once again, the motel was just at the edge of the village and everything was within walking distance. Therese smiled back thinking, when my girl is on a mission she doesn't quit. She too could not wait to find out more about the house, but as she drove to the motel, reality had come crashing down. Her stomach began to churn because she had no idea of the sale price. What if it was too high for her budget?

When checking in at reception, Therese mentioned the house to the attendant. The woman did not share much information, only that the house was up for sale and had been for many years. She also gave the oddest look, when Therese said, "that's a shame. It's a wonderful place. I love it."

Still, concern over the purchase price was on her mind. Determined and ready, Therese gathered the children and they headed for the realtor. *I'll buy it, s*he thought. *I'll find a way!*

Jade rushed forward and led the way, her footsteps moving quickly, she could not wait any longer. "You rock, Mum," announcing her compliment, as they approached the office.

The Jarrods entered the agency. Therese approached the realtor and crossed her fingers as she mentioned the house then made her offer. Then, with a much-needed exhale, Therese relaxed her formal stance and Jade joined in the celebration. Micky too began jumping and giggling, but for a completely different reason. He thought it was a party.

Therese could not believe it. Her offer was accepted without a hint of negotiation. She could afford it; she was so elated. This is just too fantastic!

The agent asked her to take a seat as he prepared documents. The kids totted over to a corner to play with some toys in a wooden box. Jade began reading some picture books to Micky, with two eyes on the book and two ears alert to the discussions held by her mother and the realtor.

The agent returned with the contracts and sat behind the desk opposite Therese, he then looked at her with an odd expression. He seemed both concerned and relieved to sell the house. He began by explaining that the current owner had previously signed all the documentation, he had never met the owner, all contact was by mail and assured Therese, that this was not the normal way he would sell a house, but this was not an ordinary circumstance.

Therese did not care, she loved it and so did Jade. The agent continued his speech, as if to deter Therese from the decision. He stated that not one local would consider buying the house, because it held the mystery of an old man's disappearance, half a century ago. Even visitors or other investors were not interested because they would hear of the tale or approach the house and feel an eerie presence. He paused as if waiting for Therese to change her mind.

"It doesn't matter to us," Therese said, breaking the silence. "We love it, we checked it out thoroughly, it needs a bit of work, and the gardens need to be tidied up, but I'm looking forward to doing it all."

The agent gasped, his face drained of all colour. "You entered the house?" he asked almost stuttering.

"Yes," she replied in a soft voice. "I'm sorry. I know I should have come here first but..." She explained the situation of their car and needing a phone.

The agent waved it off saying there was no need for an apology also adding he was glad to have a happy customer, yet his expression seemed to be one of amazement.

Just before signing, Therese looked up at the agent; then, in a curious voice asked, "What was the old man's name?"

The realtor seemed to shudder for a moment. "Medwin..." He paused as he pulled a hankie from his pocket, wiping his forehead dry from the escaping sweat. "Medwin Rune."

"Oh," Therese continued to peruse the document that lay in front of her, particularly the name of the current owner. "So Topaz Rune must be his wife."

The agent shrugged. "No one knows," he wiped his forehead again. "He was a recluse. We know very little of Medwin."

All signed, followed by cheers and a family hug, Therese and the kids returned to the motel. By now they were so hungry, Therese picked up the phone and ordered pizza. There was no time to go out for a bite. She needed to make a few phone calls and begin to devise a plan for the move to their new home; after all, it was only a five-day settlement.

"Aww," Jade whined. Five days seemed too long. She was so excited, she danced and hugged her family every few minutes. Therese and Micky joined in, they all held hands and spun in a circle singing, "we got it, we got it."

Therese had to calm herself. *So much to do*, her thoughts began flooding with tasks. Then, not waiting a moment longer, she reached for the phone and began to dial. Her adrenalin was so high she fumbled as she dialed the number of the person she could count on—her brother.

Simon Hill was a musician and jack-of-all-trades. Yet another creative member in the family, he chose to express his flair by growing his hair past his shoulders and wore hippie like clothes, justifying his outfits by saying, comfort was the key to creative expression.

"You're just like dad, you tree hugger," Therese would often say, when he vented his greenie beliefs, attempting to change the world.

He was in fact the mirror image of their father; well over six foot in height, with an attractive face carved in defined features, highlighting his pale blue eyes and strong jaw line.

Simon was the person Therese trusted above all. They had a close bond and were the best of friends; she could not wait to tell him.

The phone began to ring and within seconds, Simon answered, "hello. I knew it was you, are you there yet?"

Before Simon could say anymore, Therese blurted out the whole experience and the purchase like a formula one racing car. She even managed the whole scenario, without taking a breath. When she finished she drew in a gulp of oxygen.

"What! You bought a house?" Simon laughed as he combed his fingers through his dark brown hair.

He was only able to make out snippets of the excited outburst. It did not surprise him, though. They were both known for their spontaneity, although Simon was more thorough than his sister was, he would always assess a situation rather than jump in the deep end.

Therese managed to calm her excitement to an understandable level. She explained the events once again, then paused and said, "I need you to come here and help with the house, pleeeease. You'll love it." She knew Simon would have fun applying his skills to any handy work.

They spoke for a while longer, whilst Jade and Micky continued dancing and singing in the background, jumping on the beds, catapulting themselves all over the motel room. It was noisy, and Simon laughed as he heard the background vocals. He even joined in on some verses and occasionally he threw in jokes like, "I hope the house is sound proof or isn't there a law against repeated verses."

With the background noise increasing it was becoming difficult to continue the conversation. Simon finished, saying he would be there in three days and suggested that they all calm down a tad. He was looking forward to a chat when he arrived, but at the rate they were going, they would exhaust their vocal chords.

There was a knock on the motel door. Therese rushed to answer it, wondering who it could be. It was the pizza deliverer. With all the excitement, she had forgotten about the order. She reached for her purse, paid and even threw in a generous tip. *Share the good fortune*, she thought. The delivery man thanked her graciously then asked if she had really bought the Rune estate. Word had spread across the village.
"Yes, I sure did," Therese said with a broad grin.

He stared at her, with the same odd look as the other locals, wishing her good luck; he turned and left in a hurry.

"Why don't they just say what's on their minds?" Therese closed the door and grunted. "It's not like we don't know someone went missing, what a bunch of weirdos."

They sat down to eat and with mouths full of pizza, the atmosphere was almost serene, with the exception of chomping, and the gurgling Micky made with his drink. They all continued to feast as Therese pondered her next tasks for the big move.

Jade had just finished a mouthful of her pizza slice, ham and pineapple her favourite, when she looked at her mum.
"Do you think it's haunted?" she asked. "Maybe that's why nobody would buy it and these locals freak out."

Therese thought for a moment as she finished chomping on her mouthful.

"I don't know. I don't think so. We had the nicest feeling when we were in there remember. If anything, I'd say the house is full of angels."

Jade smiled. "Ghosts would be cool though. If there are any, I think they're nice ones."

They laughed at the thought of spooky specters. Therese was a skeptic, believing in what she could see and touch. She did not doubt that there was a higher being who created the world, but haunted houses, magic and fairytales. What a load of rubbish! Gut instinct, that's what drew her to the house. She knew it was the place they would call home.

Chapter 4

POSSESSION HAS ARRIVED

The days passed extremely slowly. The excitement and the wait made them all anxious. Micky too, though he simply just copied his mother and sister.

Each morning, not so much as a minute after opening her eyes, Jade would say, "I just want to move in today. I can't wait."

Therese was sure she had even heard Jade talking in her sleep, saying the same thing over and over again. Jade's continuous verbal impatience was wearing thin. Seriously, how many times a day could anyone cope with the same repeated sentence; Therese was getting finger cramps from pulling her hair out.

In the last three days, Simon was a great remedy; he added some variety to the wait. It had taken him only two days to sort out his work, leave, and arrive at Yarra Glen. He managed to book the motel room directly opposite the room Therese and the kids occupied. They both left the entry doors wide open, so the kids could run freely into each room, but the real reason was the fact that each room had a television. This way they could watch their favourite programs without any arguments. Micky loved his sing along ABC programs, whilst Jade loved to watch documentaries and game shows.

During the wait, Simon gathered the kids and took them on ventures around the area. This gave Therese a peaceful break to make her phone calls and cram in all her preparations. Each time they returned, the children would share their venture immediately with Therese. Simon would stand back and wait his turn, laughing at Micky's version and Jade's version of their day, including the way they both required their mother's attention. He admired his sister's patience, watching as she managed to multi-task both speeches with ease.

The kids talked about the parks, bushwalks, an arcade gallery, what they ate, the friendly people they met, the funny people they met, the animals at the pet store and showed Therese items that Simon had purchased for them. Jade chose coasters, a vase and other pieces of bric-a-brac, saying that they were all house warming presents, except for one history book, which she wasted no time in reading from cover to cover.

Micky bought bouncy balls, a plush teddy he simply named teddy, a chocolate bar he had devoured with the remnants spread across his face, and a pair of sneakers with soles that lit up each time he walked. It was difficult to see who had the most fun out on these ventures. Simon was equally as excited as the children; after all, the area was a picturesque landscape, the people were friendly, and the village had a diverse array of shops.

When they were not out exploring their new hometown, Therese and Simon sat through discussions of the tasks ahead. Jade would join in with ideas, sketches and her accustomed speech of "I can't wait". Micky entertained himself by using all the beds, including Simon's, as trampolines and spread towels in a row along the floor, spanning to each room. He used his creation as a railway track, walking back and forward from one room to the other, chugging, tooting, and laughing at his new shoes each time they lit up. He called them 'tains' meaning his train shoes. The motel staff were not ruffled at all. They laughed at Micky's invention.

Finally! It was moving day. Everyone awoke with excessive energy and excitement. With check out complete and the cars all packed, they headed to the new home, their anticipation at fever pitch. Simon had not yet seen the house, having decided to await the full experience on the big day.

They arrived at the house and Simon gasped, as his green four-wheel drive ascended the driveway to reveal the new family home. "Wow" was the only word that came out of his mouth as he inspected the enormity of the estate with a look of disbelief, only to be distracted by Jade.

"It's unreal isn't it, Uncle Simon?" she cheered.

Micky zoomed out of the car in search of the possum; Therese caught him, anxiously suggesting they go in, before they lose the little monkey in some of the overgrowth.

They headed for the front door and Jade described all aspects of the yard, then the house in detail, not missing an inch, forgetting to take a breath between sentences. Simon laughed at Jade's elaborate detail and they continued to follow Therese into the house. The children rushed upstairs, Jade in search of her new bedroom and Micky to expel more of his infinite energy. Therese gave Simon a guided tour, both suggesting many ideas for improvements to be carried out. They both made a pact to begin the very next day. Why wait when their adrenalin was rocketing?

Simon pointed out that there were no taps, with the exception of the deep round basin in the kitchen bench. The so-called tap sat to the right of the basin with a pump lever sitting over the spout. They also found there were no drain holes in any of the basins including the bathtub. The worst discovery, however, was no sign of a toilet, not even an outhouse within sight.

Therese hoped it was hidden in the yard, amongst the overgrowth. *How silly*, she thought. *I didn't think to check this the last time we were here.* Once again, she added to her 'To Do' list, and sighed before continuing the tour. She knew they would have the house up to scratch within a short period. Six months max, she told Simon. She wanted the house ready for her thirty-sixth birthday in November; and not long after hers Simon would celebrate his, only he was nine years her junior.

The next few weeks passed rapidly. Their belongings had arrived, and the children were over the moon unpacking some of the boxes, finding toys and other personal goods. Simon set up a bunk bed for the kids in the room Jade had claimed and Micky wasted no time in spreading his toys about their new bedroom.

"I can't wait till Micky's room is painted," Jade complained, grunting as she stepped over toy cars, plush animals and blocks. Thankfully, this was not permanent, and she looked forward to her own privacy, with no baby toys.

Therese decided to keep the main bedroom as it was and use the king size four-poster bed, already in place. She felt like royalty in her new bedroom, it was unique from the rest of the house with traditional designs rather than modern, except for the colour, more black, grey and white. The decorations displayed elaborate detail with carved timbers and velvet floral wallpaper. Mounted to the walls were large gilded tapestries depicting old fashioned and ancient scenes. The timber bed, canopied with heavy floral fabrics dominated the space, and a velvet chaise sat at the foot of the bed. Resting on the chaise was a white cushion; this too was centered with a black diamond. Medwin seemed to favour this shape.

The improvements on the home went full steam ahead, even Micky joined in thinking it was a game, managing to make more of a mess than there was is the first place. The possum, now a member of the family, followed Micky's example, most of the time having little or no choice, because Micky would not put it down. Micky named him Pancer, his version of Prancer, thinking it was a present from Santa.

The family mainly worked in the garden, pruning, weeding, and generally giving the yard, driveway, and pathways a good clean up. Therese contracted a plumber and electrician to carry out the tasks, on her 'To Do' list. This was a lengthy process and she had to phone outside help, because none of the local tradesmen would attend the house. They now had power, running water, and a toilet!

The gardens were cleaning up beautifully. They were able to find hidden paths, concrete sculptures and more clusters of daffodil patches across the estate. Therese even spotted a huge frog that leapt out from an overgrown bush with a long bound.

"Ahhhhh!" she bellowed. "There's a weird, giant frog. Quick! Come and look. Ooh it's gross. What the heck is it?"

They all rushed over and stared at the frog. The leather skin amphibian was a dull chocolate brown with a yellow tinge on its back, it was about the size of a small dog.

Laughing at Therese, Simon informed her that it was a cane toad. The locals advised him of the infestation and of the general size.

"They're big buggers," the nursery attendant explained, "nothing to worry about though. They're just big pests, so get rid of them if you see them."

"Oh it's so cute, mum. Can we keep him?" Jade gazed at it lovingly.

Micky also seemed to like it. He was tossing leaves and twigs over to the toad saying, "eat, fwog, nummy," and giggling.

"No way, Yuk! Its gross," Therese whined her disgust. "It'll probably give us all warts and..." before she could vent her objections further, the toad turned and with long leaps it disappeared into the overgrowth. "Anyway, he's gone now. Problem solved. Yuk!" she shuddered at the thought of a giant toad for a pet.

It had taken a few weeks, but the yard was pretty much complete. They now focused on the dining area. Their task was to pull up the tiles centered on the dining room floor and replace it with timber slats.

Eager to go, they took hold of hammers and chisels and began the demolition. Simon tested his muscles on the tough panels, pulling a strained face and grunting as he struggled with the well-glued squares that were quite thick and heavy. Therese followed his lead and removed the loosened tiles whilst she pondered their next task, the laundry.

Prancer was the culprit for the damage to the far wall in the laundry. Each day, the destructive possum scratched at the paint and tore pieces off the plasterwork. Simon tried to cover for Prancer, insisting it was only instinct.

"Possums need to maintain their claws. It's pretty much like a manicure," he said, this lame reason was an attempt to curb his sisters' anger. But this added more to their workload and Therese was not happy with the fur ball.

Suddenly, they heard a shriek. It was Jade, her voice sounded fearful. Therese stopped removing the tiles and began to bolt in a panic.

"Wow, yook, big fish," Micky screeched to his sister, pointing at the concrete pond. Jade had turned quickly in time to see a dolphin nose-dive into the pond. Her jaw dropped, and she stood, stunned.

"Muuummm!" Jade began to shout then stuttered as she relayed her experience when her Mum and Uncle rushed out to see what all the drama was about.

Simon and Therese looked at each other, then at Jade, as though she was having illusions. "No more sun for you, missy," Therese laughed.

"But, Muumm! It's true, I did see it. So did Micky," Jade whined.

However, Micky did not seem to care if there was a dolphin in the pond. He continued to run amuck creating his version of a garden masterpiece.

"It's okay, squirt," Simon reached over to rub Jade's shoulder, "I'm sure there's a logical explanation. Let's wait and see if whatever you saw jumps out again."

Both Therese and Simon knew that although Jade sometimes had an active imagination, she would never lie. It was obvious she had witnessed something, but what. They all walked over to the porch, parked their bottoms on the steps, and waited. Micky's wait was short lived; he was too restless and returned to the garden to create his version of mud pies with a salad on the side.

After a long wait, a few cups of cocoa and many subjects of conversation there was no sign of any dolphin. Simon even thoroughly inspected the pond and found it to be quite shallow. It contained nothing except for murky water, moss, and what looked quite possibly like tadpoles.

Therese hugged Jade, hoping to curb her disappointment, then called for Micky, "come on you lot, I think it's time to go inside."
Everyone entered the home, ready for dinner and to prepare for an early night.

"A dolphin," muttered Therese and chuckled to herself. "What next?"
The renovations had obviously put a strain on them all.

Chapter 5

THE GATEWAY REVEALED

Therese was up quite early the next day along with Simon who was preparing a gourmet breakfast for the kids. She needed to go to the hardware store, which was at least a thirty-minute drive, to pick up some supplies. She hopped into the car, reached for the seat belt, and nearly jumped out of her skin, when a wave of water soaked the car. Her jaw dropped, as she glimpsed the source of the splash.

"Oh...My...Gosh!" she exclaimed, pausing after each word. Jade was right!
A Dolphin had leapt into the air then nosed dived back into the pond. *That's just not possible*, she thought in a panic, still shaking from the experience.

The dolphin had disappeared in an instant. Therese jumped out of the car and ran into the house, calling out to Simon in an outburst of excitement, whilst running towards Jade's room. Bursting in on her sleeping daughter, she shook her awake, breathless as she relayed the story of the last few minutes. They were both laughing when Simon entered the room.

"Like mother, like daughter, eh. Maybe it's time both of you, lay off the sun," he chided and listened to the repeated experience then joined in the laughter. "Why not?" Simon shrugged, "first the possum, then the cane toad and let's not forget the stunt porcupine that crashed into the house after rolling downhill, boy was he disoriented. Why not a dolphin? But, this one's definitely up there in the weird book of records. Let's just leave it as super weird for now."

There was simply no logical explanation other than his sister and niece were suffering from the same delusions. But that was doubtful. Simon had inspected the pond again and this was impossible. They all headed for the kitchen in their own deep thoughts.

Therese prepared some light snacks, and Simon headed for the dining room to continue pulling up the last of the tiles. Finally, all the tiles were off, revealing a large concrete slab, about the size of a twelve-seat dining table. Simon stared for moments and began scratching his head, trying to find within his thoughts an explanation for the slab.

It doesn't make sense; this concrete block would be too heavy for this upper level, what's holding it up. Unable to find an answer, he called Therese, asking her to have a look and Jade followed. But, she too stood there thinking how odd it was to have a concrete slab in the centre of the room, on the second level, at that!

"I bet it's a grave," Jade said, with curiosity and mostly hope. "What if someone was buried in there, like that old man or something?"

Simon and Therese disagreed with her, suggesting it was probably an old verandah slab, but both secretly agreed with Jade's interpretation.

Simon left the room to collect more tools, whilst Jade continued a conversation with her mother, adamant that the slab was a hidden burial ground. Therese attempted to convince her daughter otherwise, but she was off on a tangent, as though it was a significant archeological find.

Simon returned with two sledge hammers, handed one to his sister, and they began to break the concrete. Jade stood nearby supervising with intense concentration whilst Micky remained in the kitchen munching on his vegemite sandwich and flicking the bread crusts across the room.

'What's that?" Jade hollered, over the demolition noise, she spotted an object darker than the concrete.

Simon bent over and picked up what looked like a dull metal coin at first, but it was only compressed metal with smooth sides on each face.

"Let me see," Jade was excited.

Simon handed it over, saying it was nothing but trashy metal. He continued the demolition, handing over other pieces that his niece spotted with her eagle eyes and because the colours stood out.

Jade was ecstatic with her new items and she carefully studied each one, beginning with the metal piece. Followed by the khaki patch of dried scaly skin, then the stone, which to Simon looked much like the other stones he dug up, but Jade could see a difference, it had bronze veins. The next and final piece was Jades favourite. She examined the jagged block of redwood closely. It was almost the size of her palm and contained a delicate etching of a butterfly.

All rubbish according to Simon, except for the carved wood. At least it had some interest and could be worth something. But Jade believed they all had some historical value, she ran to the lounge room and placed them on the mantel piece above the fireplace.

The demolition of the slab continued for a couple of days. Jade waited eagerly for the discovery of buried bones, but there was nothing of that sort. Therese and Simon finally completed the demolition and cleared the broken chunks of concrete, scattered where the slab once lay. They stood staring at the cavity, once again curious of the next layer embedded beneath the slab. It was a mound of coal, acting as the support, with no foundation and what made it more confusing, was that the thick layers could not be seen from the ceiling below.

"This is stupid," complained Therese. She was still puzzled and rubbed her chin in thought. "I don't get how it's attached. It's pretty thick. You'd think the room downstairs would have a lowered ceiling or something, hmm."
They all decided to take a break and work out the next plan of action, so they headed for the kitchen. Simon took hold of Micky and hoisted him up onto his shoulders. Micky giggled and squirmed stretching his arms high, aiming to reach the ceiling, tangling his uncle's hair in the process.
 Therese flicked the kettle on; she was looking forward to a cup of tea and, as she spun, caught sight of Prancer, tearing chunks off the paintwork on the laundry wall again.

"Prancer," she shouted, "you annoying possum, like we don't have enough to do without repairing your damage too."

Jade ran over to the laundry in an attempt to save Prancer from her mother's outburst. She looked at the damaged wall and began to move closer.
"Mum, there's something written underneath the paint."

Therese and Simon, with Micky still perched on his shoulders, approached the laundry. Prancer stood aside from the damaged wall, with a strange look in its eyes.

Jade began peeling off the layers of paint to reveal more of the writing. Simon reached up and guided Micky to the floor. Taking hold of his hand, they moved closer towards Jade.
Jade peeled off the last piece then edged backwards to allow full view of the writing.

The writing was in parchment script. They all studied the lines, making out each letter to help spell the words before them.

"Reveal thine forthwith the gate shall govern. Melusine Salatea Dakini," Therese read the words out aloud.

"No mum, I think the S, is a G," Jade said, and Simon began to re-read the inscription.

"Reveal thine forthwith the gate shall govern. Melusine Galatea Dakini."

Crack!!! A roaring blare pierced the house and a warm breeze of mist floated down, rapidly transforming the surroundings. Simon took firm hold of Micky, Therese took firm hold of Jade, as they watched in fascination and fear the array of colour splashing throughout the house, like paint spilling from a palate.

Abstract sculptures began to appear in every niche. The black diamond on the suspended canvas frames changed to reveal internal and external, unknown scenery. The family stood still, unable to speak and unable to take their eyes off the transformations appearing before them.

Simon opened his mouth to scream, as the metal object he had found during the demolition suddenly flew towards him with supersonic speed. He could feel the gush of wind on his neck as the object clamped onto his earlobe and embedded itself. He felt no pain only a tingle, almost like a tickle.

The others gasped, as items sped towards them, also clamping upon their ears. Therese received the scaly skin, Jade received the stone and Micky received the carved wood piece, giggling at the happenings, with no fear at all.

In less than a blink, Micky began sprouting silver lined wings, centered with tinges of glittering colours, stretching to match the length of his back. An iron cuff took formation across Simon's left wrist. He strained and pulled but was unable to remove it. A jeweled choker appeared, wrapping itself around Jade's neck. She too strained and had no success in removing it.

Therese stood waiting for her turn, but nothing appeared only the scaly skin, embedded in her earlobe. She began aiding her daughter and Simon, pulling at the attached pieces. The cuff felt light, in fact, Simon could not feel it at all and Jade felt the same with her choker. Micky was gleeful, running in circles, reaching behind him trying to touch his new wings. They all continued their attempts to remove the accessories, when they heard a voice.

"Stop it. No matter how much you try, they cannot be removed."

"Oh... My...Gosh!" A choir of each voice bellowed at the sight. Micky screeched with excitement, stretching out his arms ready for a hug.

"Why, thank you, Micky," Prancer said and gave an odd bow, looking at Micky with adoring eyes, "I do appreciate the love and affection. He is quite a good boy, somewhat active, but very good just the same."
Therese, Simon and Jade could not fathom this. The plump possum was speaking!

"What's happening?" Therese was pale and shook her head as though this would bring everything back into focus.

"Please try to refrain yourself for a moment. I understand this must been quite an experience for all of you. I shall explain, but I wish to begin by thanking you all for opening the gateways."
Therese, Simon, and Jade looked at each other, the house, then back to the possum.
"There is no need for concern, in regard to your surroundings. Medwin and I lived this way before he disappeared. I can assure you it is quite safe."

Jade felt her excitement grow. "Wow, you knew the old man, and this was his place back then," she said. "It's unreal, it's the bomb."

Prancer studied the notion for a moment. "Yes, it is rather unreal," the furry creature said, stumbling over the last word. "Medwin is very mighty in sorcery and he was able to create his own world of colour, amusement, and mysticism, within this house. The black and white you saw previously, was simply a balance of yin and yang harmony, created to conceal the true form."

Prancer edged closer to the intrigued family.

"Simon you have opened the gateways and recreated Medwin's way of life when you spoke the incantation written on the wall. There are a few differences though, I must add."

The family huddled together, ready to absorb more of the unbelievable information as they studied the possum and their surroundings.

"The objects of power you have been awarded were hidden by my master many years before. I have long awaited the day when the bearers would receive them. It was with much effort I planned your arrival and aided in your destiny to find this house." Prancer paused looking at each family member like a proud parent.

They all stood still, pondering in wonder except for Micky, he was still trying to catch his wings. "I knew there was something that drew me to this house," Therese said, her voice a little shaky. "But I don't understand why!' she asked in a roundabout way.

"Come along, we shall retire to the living room and discuss what you need to know," the possum prompted with its claw and began to walk across the kitchen. "By the way," it turned, looking back at the family, "my name is Topaz, though I did find the name Prancer quite amusing. It is a pleasure to meet you formally."

Topaz bowed her head and continued her walk.

Chapter 6

RUTHLESS DESCENDANTS

The family followed Topaz with eyes darting all around the house. It was amazing! Every wall was a different colour, in blues, greens, oranges, reds, and yellows. It was bright and fun.

Spellbinding colours, objects, and a talking possum had opened their view to expect the unexpected, but more added surprises came into focus, when they passed the entry points into the bedrooms and bathroom.

They found themselves laughing and having a joyous time as they chatted with some doors and greeted others. Each door was unique in colour and had come alive, enabling each to move quite freely as though they were made of soft rubber. They portrayed faces with all sorts of expressions; this made it easy to determine some of their personalities, however there were some tricky ones too. Even the furniture greeted them and aided the family on the walk toward the living room.

"This is fun," Jade laughed when a chair slid beneath her acting as an escort.

Her guide zoomed off and pretended to be a bumper car as it crashed into other furniture. The disgruntled furniture acted on impulse and returned the favour with a whack to the chair, most missed though.

They were all present in the lounge room now. Micky tried with much difficulty to break the embrace Simon had on him. The stairway leading to the lower level had transformed into a giant water slide, with spouts of water shooting sprinkles all the way down the edges and ending in a pool of water. This water semi filled the downstairs area. The pool looked so inviting that Micky began gnawing on his uncle's forearm in the hope of freedom and a chance to play on the slide. No luck though, Simon locked his grip.

Topaz stopped then pointed a claw towards the lounge suite asking each of them to take a seat in a static voice, she spoke impeccable English. With a rapid motion, the sofa, recliner, and armchair swooped over, gliding beneath Therese, Simon, and Topaz, until they were seated comfortably. The recliner insisted on adjusting itself, until Simon was completely satisfied in a relaxed position; then, with its lever, it took hold of Micky's wing halting him in flight, relieving Simon from any distraction.

Jade, already seated in her dodgem chair, laughed as she watched her mother and uncle fumble with their seats. She also watched Micky as he continued his fight for freedom, thinking, *he's got the right idea. I'd love to go for a swim and down the awesome water slide.*

Topaz cleared her throat then adjusted herself to an erect stance. "I shall begin by firstly saying, welcome. I have spent much time in thought of this moment. I cannot thank you all enough; I am very pleased to finally see the gateways open. It is now the beginning, to the end."

The family listened intently, as Topaz began by introducing her good friend and master, Medwin, followed by an explanation of his disappearance.

"Medwin believed he was called upon to aid a friend in need," she paused for a moment and her expression saddened, "only to find a well-planned enticement that lured him into the hands of Mulgot and Rosmer, two power starved Sylphs, who have burning desires to control all paths of life. Though they possess minimal magical abilities, these two operate with cold approach and intense hatred. They aim to achieve their goals at any expense."

"Uh... what, s.i.l.f," Jade spelled out each letter, trying to recall the word in a dictionary. "What's a silf?" she asked, rubbing her ears thinking she had misheard.

"It is Sylph, ph no f," replied Topaz. "They are descendants of Fairies but were banished from the communities because of their fierce competitiveness along with their unstable temperaments. They performed all tasks with malicious cruelty and self-gained thoughts. They are not at all like their relatives."

Sylphs came to be when a handful of fairies morphed with mosquitoes. This race lives many hundreds of years, but age is not against them. They are very handsome creatures, with sharply defined features, long narrow violet eyes, and petite upturned noses. They are very humanlike in many aspects, but they are taller and possess greater strength. Their skin is moth like, with tufts of dull brown fur embodied on their torso. Though possessing minimal power, their sting can hypnotize a victim allowing full mind control. They also have the ability to fly aided by transparent sword-like wings that span farther than the length of their body. No one knows the whereabouts of this race but Medwin and other world inhabitants have had the displeasure of meeting the only two sighted in many years, Mulgot and Rosmer.

"Enough about that, where were we?" Topaz looked up towards the ceiling in search of her thoughts, "Oh yes" she continued, "Medwin and I entered the gateway and realised it was a trap. Mulgot and Rosmer attempted to enter this world to obtain certain items. These five items would give them power in the human world, and with their accumulated knowledge they would succeed with control. Medwin immediately reacted in haste. Knowing the gateways were exposed, he propelled me back through and sealed his exit, unable to return, also trapping the Sylphs with him. The only way to reopen any of the gateways, is from the opposite side, this world, and not many are worthy of this task, until now."

Topaz paused, lost in her own memories, then without warning, she changed the subject, "And now, four of the items for power have been obtained, already in your possession. They are the bewitched objects discovered upon your dig."

The possum studied the family sitting before her and continued addressing each of them in turn.

"Simon, you have received the iron cuff from the metal. This contains the sweat of Zeus and grants you immense strength. Jade you have received the choker of gems from the rock. This contains the energy of life granting you the power to heal and Micky," Topaz looked at her little friend and smiled, "has sprouted wings. Perhaps this is not a great gift for such a lively toddler but nevertheless, his carved wood contains a feather from a unicorn wing and he has been granted the obvious, flight. And Therese, even though there is no visible accessory, you have received the scaly skin containing the blood of a chameleon. This grants you the power of camouflage."

All but Micky sat before Topaz with the same thoughts, eyes scanning all the visible areas of the room.

"Ok, where's the candid camera?" Simon asked with obvious sarcasm. "Ha ha very funny and a talking scatter brain possum. Good one."

Topaz was not surprised at the disbelief; she pointed a claw at Micky. "Answer this, how does a child sprout wings?"

"Illusions, wires, and animatronics for the furniture," Jade was quick to respond, finding it improbable for any of it to be real, but secretly hoping it was.

"I can assure you, Jade, there are no tricks of mastery here," said Topaz. "It is very real and now it is also a part of all your being."

Jade cheered, it did not take much to convince her of the reality. "It's unreal, I really, really, really love it. See, mum, I knew the house was cool."

Therese laughed at Jade's excitement, then looked at Simon who was in deep thought, still trying to work it out.

"I know what you're thinking, Simon. How could this possibly be real? But look around, it is. We can't justify it. I don't particularly want to or know how. We were drawn here and with that, we're lucky to see a world that's hidden from our reality. Come on step outside the square, there's more to life than tree hugging."

Simon looked back intently and nodded in agreement. "You're right, sis, but if Medwin is locked in with those creature things, Musgot or whatever, then everything is safe because they can't get out, Right?" he asked turning to Topaz.

"Not precisely, dear Simon," Topaz sighed with concern. "There are other evil beings and the most horrific of all is the ability Mulgot has of possibly breaking down Medwin and absorbing some of his powers, giving these awful Sylphs the ability to escape their prison through another dimension."

"WHAT?" snapped Simon, "So they can get out through another door?"

Topaz nodded. "That is correct. Let us just hope that Medwin still has his strength to contain them. And fortunately now, Medwin can have your aid."

Simon's jaw was gaped in horror, then he perked up, a brave force taking hold. "Okay. I'm outside the square, I can be a hero," he flexed his muscles playfully. "I'm not sure what we can do but bring it on. I'm ready for the ride! But…" he began to smirk. "I'll still stick with tree hugging too."

Topaz sunk back into the armchair rattling a long sigh of relief.

They all began to test their new powers, when Topaz interrupted "These gifts of power cannot be forced. Only Micky can use his power of flight, unbeknownst to him and only when they are understood or called upon in need will they reveal themselves. You will know when the time is upon you."

Simon's thoughts still pondered the previous conversation he needed an answer. "If the Sylphs can escape, why did you let us to re-open the gateways?"

"I expected this question," replied Topaz, "my youth is escaping. I do not know how long I am capable of deterring your kind from this house and as I stated before there are other evil beings."

"Oh," Therese was not really listening to what Topaz had said, her mind focused elsewhere. "So where is the fifth item?" she asked, disappointed with the delay of her new-found power.

"That is what you must seek," the possum looked up at the ceiling to jog her memory. "Oh yes! The entry is upon the coals."

Therese stared at Topaz in confusion, "what coals?" then she remembered the mess of the excavation. "You don't mean that mound in the dining room?"

Topaz smiled with a static growl, they all leapt up and darted towards the dining room.

Chapter 7

A PUZZLING STATE OF AFFAIRS

The family was not prepared for the enormity of what lay before them. It was a huge board, the length of a cricket pitch. The coals had melted forming glowing red outlines of a jigsaw puzzle with eight missing puzzle pieces.

Topaz followed. Taking the lead, she leapt onto the board. It was cool, yet it gave the impression of hot coal. Therese, Simon and Jade were busily feeling the surface when the possum expelled a loud rattle to gain attention.

"You must enter the gateway to each world, seek the piece and return it to its place. When all the pieces are complete this will open the dimension for the fifth item and will also be the gateway towards the world where Medwin is trapped."

Jade jumped on the board. It felt as though she was standing on a hard rubber mat with little bounce. "This feels weird," she giggled, "but where are the gateways?" Her enthusiasm began to stir.

"They are every internal door you see," Topaz pointed a claw toward the direction of these entries that were once the solid black doors etched with white numbers.

"Cool," Jade cheered and danced across the board, Micky joined in. "I can't wait. What an adventure!" They all were eager to begin.

The family searched the house and began heading towards the purple door when Topaz leapt in front of them, her fur spiked with fright.

"Halt, you cannot enter that one, not yet that is. You must go through each door in numerical order; otherwise, it could force a disastrous effect. I just don't recall what occurs." Topaz explained the connection of the white digits on each black door, before the gateways were revealed.

Listen to the possum; they all agreed in unison, the possum knows best. We hope!

"Ok, so door number one is our first target, umm," Simon chewed on his bottom lip as he thought. "I wish I'd paid more attention to the doors before. Which one was it?"

Jade was bouncing, she raised her arm and waved it about to distract Simon from his thoughts. "I know, I know. It's mum's room. I remember it."

Therese grunted in agreement. It was her turn to pin Micky down. With great effort, she held onto his ankles as he fluttered the wings, attempting to zoom off on his own adventure. Simon relieved Therese. His arm tingled, and he could feel a fraction of his newfound strength. He was able to hold Micky with ease.

They headed for door one and stopped inches from the rubbery entry to analyse it before they pondered the next step.
"Should we knock?" Therese asked, as the yellow door laughed, entertaining itself with jokes.

The door paused then looked directly at the family and asked, "Password?"

"Password, what password!" Therese began a spin to seek advice from Topaz when the door interrupted.

"Only joking." it giggled. "I am the way to the world of delightful desires. Turn my handle anti-clockwise and enter."
They did and stopped at the sight before them.
"Go on then, you'll be fine," urged the door and they began their journey.

A few steps through the gateway, they could hear Topaz call out. "Do not forget to close the door. Unexpected visitors are not always a welcome sight. After all, I think we have enough occupants."

Topaz a very intelligent possum by far, occasionally suffered memory lapses and quite often spoke before her brain was able to make sense of it. Medwin called them her dizzy moments and gained much joy during these occasions. Her verbal trips were not because of her accumulated age, it was purely a gift from birth making her more loveable not just for her large black eyes and soft pink nose.

Simon pulled the door toward him, closing any sight of Topaz and their house, thinking of the last comment. *Occupants, I hope she doesn't mean us!*

"Oh dear," Topaz said to herself and shuddered, after the door was closed. "I forgot to mention what occurs when they take hold of the puzzle piece."
She hoped they all were quick enough to survive the experience.

Chapter 8

THE MYTHICAL THEME PARK

They stood on a rainbow high above an expanse of clear blue sky. There was nothing below them and nothing beside them. The path was overlapping primary colours of red, yellow and blue with defining shades of orange, green and purple. Simon moved forward to test the surface. It looked like a long cloud of smoke, but a few steps revealed the surface to be firm and every step had left indents on the surface. Within seconds, the dimples bounced up and returned to their original state. Simon's concern turned to relief. "It's okay. We won't fall through," he reached over and took hold of Micky.

Therese had Micky in her care once again allowing Simon to test the waters. She embraced Jade around the shoulders, ready to grip tighter in the event of the unknown, and they all began to progress forward.

The rainbow path continued for what seemed like a mile, straight and consistent all the way, until they reached the edge. Open skies with no other surface brought them to a standstill, yet in the distance, they could see a miniature city of skyscrapers and highset bridges.

"Great, what now?" Jade dropped her posture to a slump.

"I don't know. Umm. Maybe we just keep walking, or maybe do a long jump," suggested Simon. He smirked at his last comment.

"A really, really, big long jump," Therese chuckled.

Simon stretched his free hand out for Therese to take hold. Using his right leg only, he stepped off the edge and lost balance as he dropped. The force tore away the grip Therese had on his hand dropping her onto the surface. Micky was able to free himself from the grip of her other hand. He began spinning and darting in the air, above his mother. Jade screamed in fear, as she saw her uncle fall.

"Uncle Simon, No.o.o!" Tears streamed out of her eyes and continued when she saw Simon's hand grip the edge of the rainbow, pulling himself up with ease.

"This new strength is a bonus," he smiled as he stood up.
Jade ran over and gripped tightly around his waist, shaken from the fear of losing her uncle.

"I'm okay, squirt." He returned a hug, looking over at Therese. "Maybe that's not the way across." He jerked when he heard his nephew squeal.

Micky started a giggle calling out "Bubbloos" as blisters of foam began to surround them. Simon, Therese and Jade looked about searching for the place that had released the bubbles when they spotted the ascending clouds that now appeared.

The clouds were shooting bubbles in every direction like raindrops, only they rose up not down, they were being showered in bubbles that multiplied to millions. Micky and Jade screeched with delight and began a popping frenzy, laughing at the twinkling sound each burst made.

"Yuk! They're sticky." Jade said and stretched her tongue in disgust, laughing as she spun in circles, aiming to pop many in one hit.

They all became saturated in this sticky substance and felt an odd lightweight sensation. Their bodies began to lift, gently floating, when a face appeared, morphing out of the rainbow path. It was the face of door one. Before they could speak, it drew back a deep breath then exhaled with great force. The gust gathered the family, propelling them towards the city; an echo of laughter filled the air as they floated rapidly and somersaulted in all directions.

"Whooo Hoooo. What a buzz," Simon's voice reverberated along with gleeful cheers from the others.

Nearing the edge of the city, once again the face appeared above them, camouflaged within the pale blue sky. It released another deep breath, exhaling a gust of hot air this time, forcing them to float down, towards the surface of the city. They could feel the breath dry their wet clothes and stared wide eyed at the landing destination. It was a large silver pot, full of what looked like gold; the family dropped smoothly into the pot and found it to be an unexpected surprise.

"This must be the much-desired pot of gold," Simon laughed. He fed some violet crumble into his mouth and mumbled, "Yum! No wonder everyone wants to find it."

They all joined in for the taste test when a voice interrupted their feast.

"Welcome you are. Bendis, my name is, a waited pleasure you to meet, now all you, fun to have, please me you follow."

A fuzzy, red haired dwarf, with a beard to match, appeared wearing a frilled yellow suit with a matching top hat. His body was round, like a pile of car tyres. This made his arms and legs look out of proportion. He bowed then turned and began to waddle towards their next destination.

The family arose and followed him.

"He talk's weird, mum. What's he saying?" Jade asked.

They all were confused with his odd choice of sentencing.

"I think he was expecting us and wants us to have some fun," Simon hoped he was right.

Bendis stood by a row of carriages and opened the side panels on a toy train parked at the foot of the pot.

"In jump all you," he ordered.

They stared at him, it was a toy train, made of plastic, they would be lucky to get a foot in. This guy was out of his mind.

The dwarf headed for the first cabin, he then placed his foot on top of the carriage and they all gaped in wonder, when instantly, the carriage grew to a size just fit to accommodate his body.

"On, come," Bendis waved his chubby little hand impatiently towards the other cabins.

"Ok, here goes."

Simon was first to attempt by placing his toe on a carriage and sure enough, it expanded just enough to suit his body. Therese and Jade followed suit, but Micky fluttered to the front steam funnel, held on, and began tooting as the train started to move along the tracks with no driver. The width of the tracks grew, taking shape of each carriage and narrowed for the vacant cabins attached to the rear, they were still the size of a toy.

Other than Micky's noises, the train ride was silent. Therese watched in concern, unable to reach him. Pouring out the funnel was suds of foam, covering her baby boy like a snowman. This did not bother Micky at all. He was tooting and singing all the way to their destination, even when they broke through a glass curtain that shattered into thousands of pieces. Thankfully, no one received so much as a scratch from the shattered glass.

The train passed through the broken wall and the family watched as the glass automatically repaired itself in reverse motion. Everyone was amazed except for Bendis and there was more.

Therese, Jade, and Simon gaped at the views around them they were awe struck. This was not what they had expected. The far city was in fact a mass carnival of rides, side shows, and crowds of unusual characters. But, not what they would call normal. The train came to a stop and Bendis waved his hand directing them off board. They all climbed out then watched the carriages shrink back to a toy.

"Wow, it just gets cooler," Jade said, and she ran to her mum, throwing her arms around her waist.

Micky zoomed over to join his sister; both embraced their mother, as if it was Christmas. Therese returned the hugs laughing and began wiping suds off Micky's face with her sleeve as he aided, blowing raspberries to clear the foam from his mouth. Suddenly, she felt flutters running up her torso and was startled when a tiny creature holding a cloth, leapt off her shoulder onto Micky, frantically wiping off all the remaining suds. The creature then backtracked all the way down, disappearing only to leave a glimpse of fur. Micky giggled and waved to the creature then positioned his head onto his mother's chest. He fell asleep within seconds.

Simon had turned his observation to the crowd in a line up, waiting for the train. They were people just like themselves, only their skin and hair mimicked colours of the rainbow. Not only were they in the line, they were everywhere, orange people with red hair, blue people with yellow hair, and purple people with blue hair, even the surroundings followed the colours, including multicoloured trees with green or blue bark.

"Pardon, you must, fun you have." Bendis bowed and was gone in an instant.

"What now?" Therese looked at Simon.

"Maybe we're supposed to go on the rides to find that puzzle piece," Jade suggested, smiling up at her mother with flickering eyes. She hoped so anyway.

"Well, it sounds like a plan," agreed Simon. "Let's go."

They stepped deeper amidst the carnival, staring at the side shows and rides before them. The staff all over this land was not like the majority crowd. There was a leathery skinned giant with a matted afro of murky mustard hair, operating the Ferris wheel. He stood beside the large contraption, asking the riders how fast they would like to go, in a kindly distorted voice. His large nose covered in warts kept hitting his top lip, vibrating each word. He then took hold of the structure and spun it like a lucky wheel.

Another giant held out an outstretched finger, spinning a suspended pirate ship containing screaming people. There were bodies falling out in every direction, but the giant reached to his side and pulled a tree from its roots, shaking elephant ear leaves off the branches until they floated beneath the falling bodies, catching them and zooming off like flying carpets. Still holding the remnants of the tree, he bit off chunks, eating it like celery. A brutish looking Cyclops stood near this giant only she was slightly shorter than her co-worker, crowds ran towards the one-eyed beast, throwing themselves into the tangled slime green rope that she tossed about like a yo-yo. When the ride was over, she peeled each body off, releasing them because they were stuck to the gluey substance

"Gosh! Look," Jade was shocked and pointed to a tall structure.

This was the bridge they had seen from the distance, but close up it was a roller coaster and nothing but a death trap. The contraption was made entirely of dominoes, stacked hundreds of meters high and appeared to be on the edge of collapse with an incomplete track that stopped at a huge gap. A banshee, with tangled hair, long grey teeth and withered skin expelled a frightening screech whilst she operated the rickety ride. Therese, Simon and Jade watched in terror as a single coaster car made of iron was screaming along the track and neared the unfinished edge. They all gasped, watching the car fly off then float over to a large waterslide opposite. The car began to transform into a watertight capsule as it flew, then dropped, crashing into the water below. Even the water was visible, appearing as a cliff wall about ninety feet in height with no supports, revealing the capsule floating like a submarine as sea life swam around it, then a massive sea serpent emerged, gulping the capsule with ease.

"That's four rides I don't want to go on," Jade said, voicing her concern.

There were so many rides.
People sat on giant ladybeetles that scurried about bumping into each other, apologising after each bump. A ghost train, haunted and operated by real ghosts was a definite no go for Jade, because the spirits invaded

the riders to possess their bodies. Giant squids with people suctioned to the tentacles, spun with extreme speed. A merry-go-round rotated as it floated inches from the ground, with real unicorns and a smaller version with foals, for the younger children. An automatic playground with swings and seesaws moved with voice activation, and a slide flipped up or down depending on where the child was. A tall, chunky troll with rock-like skin, operated a canon and blasted people through a hole in the sky, teleporting them to other holes on the ground. The flying swing that looked safe at first, was put in motion, and the ropes stretched, throwing the riders in all directions of the park.

Simon's face paled as he watched the on goings. He enjoyed the adrenalin rush from carnival rides, but these were too extreme, even for him.

There were neon signs floating above all the rides that flashed and chanted except for one that burped belly-go-round. It was a merry go round with giant fruit. People boarded this ride and bit large chunks out of the fruit to create a seating area. When the ride had finished, giant worms squirmed out of the fruit, devouring the produce, until it disappeared and a new one appeared in its place.

"Yuk! There's no way I'm going on that one." Therese gagged at the thought of worm filled fruit.

A tall and wide building full of mazes, rocked as though it was ready to fall. Another tall building with springs along the bottom edges was surrounded with bouncing people, attempting to jump through the highest window to win a prize. The prizes were little fluffy live creatures, slimy lizard like creatures, and temporary spells. There was even lava erupting from a volcano, with people surfing and boogie boarding down its façade towards families swimming in the molten lake.

Micky's favourite were the scatters of jumping castles, housing young children leaping in high bounds all over the carnival. Jade liked the stilts. The tall rubbery poles walked about freely and tapped customers, sometimes whacking them across the head, inviting them to jump on. They made her laugh. The dwarf jugglers were also a favourite. Both Jade and Micky giggled as they watched the jugglers toss bearded little garden gnomes that yelped and cursed in grumpy voices. The complaints were for lack of height or lame juggling, not because they were the objects. The sideshows were just as odd as the rides.

A row of dwarf clowns, standing along the edge of a platform, opened their mouths each time a child placed ping-pong balls in them. The clowns began to choke, their faces glowed a bright red followed by hiccups. The hiccups revealed the amount of points each ball received.

There was a shooting gallery with live silver geese. The birds scampered about dodging each pellet that headed towards them and the disgruntled players walked away complaining the game was rigged. Another sideshow people whined about was the fishing game. Players were casting rods at the ninety-foot wall of water and a prize could only be won if the serpent was caught, but the beast was clever and avoided the lures.

There were squids, making balloon animals, transforming the completed balloons into live miniature animals whilst wart infested, Hob Goblins shape shifted into the same animals, entertaining the onlookers but they were still covered in the same warts.

Cats and dogs were a favourite; these people were in awe, as though these pets were rare.

More dwarfs, male and female, both with beards, in all shapes and sizes walked on air, pushing food and novelty trolleys. They served purple beverages with suds, rainbow fairy floss attached to wands held by tiny fairies, foods that seemed to bite back, self-cleaning wands, toys that moved and talking show bags. The bags promoted themselves, advising carnival goers of the goodies contained within.

"Wow, wow, wow, this place is..." Therese stopped, searching for a description, "different." That was the best she could think of at the moment. "I'm exhausted, it's bizarre overload, I just want to sit down for a while and work out how to find the puzzle piece." She was still holding a sleeping Micky in her arms and the weight was escalating.

A yellow bench came zooming over, sliding itself beneath Therese.

"Watch it," squealed a squeaky voice.
Therese leapt up, gripping Micky tighter and was faced by a round ball of fluff with velvet thin, long arms, tiny hands and legs to match. It jumped up and opened its mouth wider than its body, squealing,
"you nearly squashed me, you did. Can't you see this bench is dirty, it is," snapped the creature, still rapidly wiping the mess. The ball of fur finished its clean up then scurried off.

"What was that?" Therese asked or should she say, what were they!

These tiny creatures were everywhere, scurrying about in speedy steps, cleaning up the grounds and picking up litter, even rushing to pick up litter as it was dropping. They were only two inches high but managed to carry large pieces of rubbish above their head as they scurried away to dispose of it. They looked like golf balls covered in mink fluff with large oval eyes and tiny pink noses that jutted out from the centre of their round bodies. Each one had different coloured arms and legs with bodies in shades of light golden browns. Their palms covered in tiny goose bumps acted as suctions to climb any height.

"Pickwicks, they are," an approaching dwarf answered. "Janitors and takers of care they are, polite always they are, angry not always they are." This Dwarf had fuzzy blue hair, he was chubbier than the others and wore red overalls with a yellow frilled shirt that matched his bowler hat. "Bendis Mister send he Jiba. On go you, sling swing, you fun have. Better you for."

"A what, a sling swing?" asked Simon, "It sounds dangerous. Where's Bendis? We need to find a puzzle piece. Can you help us?"

The dwarf shook his head, "Jiba help cannot, Jiba no not where, Bendis Mister help."

"Okay, so where can we find him?" Simon asked with gritted teeth.

"Say, Bendis Mister, you fun have, sling swing," Jiba smiled, his mouth full of large square teeth.

It was impossible. There was no straight answer.

"Fine!" snapped Simon. "We'll go on this fun thing and then can we see Bendis?"

But the dwarf bowed and disappeared in an instant.

"Why does everyone just disappear?" Simon asked, not really expecting an answer. "Well, let's do it. Sling swing here we come."

Simon reached for Micky, giving Therese's arms a break. Micky began to stir, which worked out quite well; Simon had the strength to stop him from flying off.

The family walked through rows all over the carnival in their search. Jade stopped and begged to enter an arcade building she had spotted, Therese agreed, and they entered, viewing the activity.

The virtual reality games had the characters jumping out of the screen, acting out the mission with the player. There were three D car games that pulled the driver through the screen. There were video screens of pinball, puzzlers, action and fantasy games wallpapered on all walls. Jade watched with excitement each time someone jumped through a screen and began physically playing the game. Simon offered to play some, but Therese and Jade were not as keen, simply because they were not sure how to end them. They exited the arcade and continued the search for the Sling swing.

The family trekked through the carnival, checking every neon sign nearby and as far as their eyes reached, then finally they spotted the flashing lights of the ride.

"Whoo Hoo," they all cheered then made a path for the Sling Swing and saw Bendis standing beside it, as they neared.

"He can't be serious," Therese stated in shock. "I'm not letting the kids on that." She grabbed Jade tightly and reached over at Simon to clutch Micky's hand.

It was a giant catapult, made of the same metal as the coaster car.

Bendis bowed as they approached. From the look on Therese's face, he could see her concern and confirmed, "Safe it is, worry you not."

This did not relieve her panic. "Sure," she replied in a sarcastic tone. "Look Bendis, I know you want us to have some fun, but we just want to find the puzzle piece and avoid any bodily harm."

Bendis smiled, "know I do, on rainbow you seek, embedded it is."

"What!" It was Jade's turn for frustration. "You mean it was on the rainbow all the time?"

Bendis nodded, "right you are, sit, you must, rainbow you will go," then he pointed his chubby little finger at the seat, on the end of the catapult.

"But," Therese cut in ready to voice her concerns again.

Bendis reached up and rubbed her lower back repeating, "Safe, you will be."

She shrugged and led her family to the seat. What choice did they have?

All seated, Therese embraced Jade and Micky tightly. Simon sat behind with his arms gripping his sister and the children. Clunk! They heard the lever release, sending them plummeting up towards the rainbow, in slow motion. It was fun, almost like their trip down, only calmer.

They reached the edge of the rainbow, their feet landing smoothly.

"That was unreal, mum. We should do it again," suggested Jade.

"No way," replied Therese, "Let's get this puzzle piece and get out of here."

They scanned the path until Jade spotted the piece embedded in the path, only metres from the exit door. Simon reached down and lifted the piece up with ease when suddenly, they felt a tremor below their feet. The rainbow began splitting at every joint and melted along the edges.

"Not good," Simon shouted over the cracking noise, "Ruuun."

They sprinted for the door, Simon last, pulling his foot in time of the final collapse. He slammed the door shut and they all stood there for a few minutes, catching their breath.

Simon regained his composure then turned to reopen the door. He was curious to see what had occurred. The face on the door had gone. It was now a normal solid yellow. He reached down turning the handle, the door opened revealing Therese's bedroom once again, but with colours of rich reds, golds, and chocolates. The gateway was gone.

"Sorry", they could hear the rattling sound of Topaz, approach, "I forgot to mention the pathways will collapse when you have the puzzle piece in possession." She was relieved to see them in fine order and began rubbing herself along Jade's leg with a show of affection.

"That's fine…NOT!" snapped Simon, then calmed as he continued, "Is there anything else we need to know?" He inhaled slow, deep breaths.

"Yes," replied Topaz, "But first, you must place that piece in the correct position."

They walked over to the puzzle board, finding the outline of the piece Simon laid it in place and watched as it lit up, mimicking the glow of the red outline.

"Now, let's have a chat," demanded Simon as he let go of Micky allowing him to flutter freely in every direction.

Therese laughed and watched her son closely, she was not overly excited with his power of flight, he was active enough without the wings, this just made him more footloose, and she was exhausted just thinking about it. Micky flew about in a giggle, holding one arm behind his back. Therese became alarmed. "Oh no! I think Micky's hurt!"

Chapter 9

THE SELF-SUSTAINING ORCHARDS

They all began jumping about to catch Micky in flight. Simon succeeded, taking hold of his arm to see if there was any damage.

Micky tugged and squirmed, enclosing a tight left fist, he repeated, "mine."

There was a tuft of fur jutting out from the cracks of his fingers. Simon peeled back all fingers at once, revealing a shaken Pickwick with turquoise coloured arms, legs, and eyes to match.

"Oh, it's so cute," Jade said and reached over gently touching it with her finger.

The fur was like melted butter, so soft, she began tenderly scratching the top of its head in an attempt of comfort. But this did not relax the Pickwick at all. It reacted with an over excited, spasmodic giggle and frantically tossed its arms and legs about in a fit.

Topaz rattled an awkward laugh; the giggle was contagious. "They do love a head scratch," she regained her composure. "It affects them as a tickle, hence the wild laughter."

Jade stopped, allowing the tiny creature to calm itself as well as the rest of her family, they too were laughing.

Topaz shook her head, "oh dear, we now have another occupant. However, we should be grateful

Micky has chosen a Pickwick and not something else. These creatures are gentle and very helpful. They are polite most often, it is only on rare occasions they show their anger, particularly if one interferes or stops them from their tasks. They are the caretakers and menders in many gateways, small enough to enter the tiniest gaps and are one of the most welcomed creatures in all worlds, but, sometimes a little over eager with cleanliness."

"No we's not," squeaked a tiny voice.

The Pickwick was also listening, as it scurried up Micky's neck, ready to wipe his dirty face, "we is clean, that's all," it began to frantically wipe Micky's chin, then scurried back down to the floor and looked at Topaz. "Me wants to go home, me does." Its wide oval eyes beginning to well. "Me mammy and me duddy, they be worried, they will, not finding their boy."

"But, the gateway is closed," Therese said and looked at Topaz in the hope of a resolution.

Topaz nodded then responded in a sad voice, "Yes, that is correct; you cannot return home." She looked at the teary Pickwick his nose quivering from the sob. "The only way you can return is to find Medwin. He will know how to re-open the gateway."

"It's okay, Pickwick," Jade reached down and took a gentle hold resting him in the palm of her hand, hoping to cheer him up. "We'll take care of you until we find the old dude."

Old dude. Humph! Children today. Topaz cringed at Jade's description of Medwin.

Pickwick looked up at Jade, his fountain of tears coming to a halt. He felt safe in Jade's care. He scurried over to her pinky finger and embraced it with his skinny arms. "Pickwick help you, me will, and you help Pickwick," he squeaked and continued the cuddle.

Jade was ecstatic. She had gained a new pet and there was no way any of her friends had one like this. Therese and Simon were also happy, after all, it was very cute and it liked to clean. What a bonus! There was a choir of grumbles. All the action of the trek had expelled much of their energy leaving them famished. A feast and a rest were in order.

"The chat can wait." Therese said. "I'm starving."

"Me too," Jade, Simon and Micky concurred.

"I agree," replied Topaz. "I too, could eat a barrel full of apple soup."

"Yuk!" exclaimed Jade, sticking her tongue out in disgust. "Apple soup! Who eats apple soup, and besides don't possums eat raw food, leaves and some meat?"

Topaz rolled her eyes. "Humans," she rattled and shook her head. "You have no idea when it comes to good food. Medwin and I always made it fresh, after collecting the juiciest apples from the orchard. What really makes my fleas crawl is the idea of canned pet food." Topaz shuddered at the thought. "Humans believe their pets enjoy that awful processed meat. Myself as do many other pets enjoy a cuisine of natural vegetation. Have you not seen a dog or cat eat grass, hmm? Humans conclude that it is for a medicinal purpose. Balderdash! Fruit and vegetables, added in delicious recipes, this is what we want." Topaz rubbed one claw on her stomach closing her eyes in heavenly thoughts. "Mmm apple soup, without forgetting a squeeze of lime and a sprinkle of sea salt, of course."

They all followed suit with Jade poking tongues out in disgust.

"Orchard?" Therese asked. "What orchard. Are there fruit trees on this estate?"

Topaz smiled. "Oh my dear, our lessons continue. Things are not as they appear, as you know by now. The canvas frames you see about the house are not purely pictures but are the doorways to Medwin's way of life. He created these rooms for his everyday needs."

Therese headed for a nearby painting followed closely by the family. She stared at the pictured frame before her and slowly guided her hand through the canvas. It was a room! filled with everyday groceries such as dairy foods, produce, toiletries, and to Jade's and Micky's excitement, a candy corner.

"So, that's why they hang so low. To step inside?" she asked Topaz, who nodded in agreement. Therese walked to the opposite side of the frame finding the same store, only a back view.

Some of the artworks were double sided, with a different store or room, others were the same as the general store with back views only. There was a furniture store with a workshop, a science lab full of odd gadgets, a clothing boutique equipped with racks housing all sorts of outfits for men, women, and children, and a bathroom with running water, drains, and a toilet. *That explains it*, Therese thought. No wonder there was no toilet in the house.

"Now," Topaz stopped for a moment forgetting her thoughts. "Oh, that was it. All ready, shall we collect lunch?" They all stared, "from the orchard of course," Topaz added to curb the confused expressions, "there are wonderful fruit trees, strawberry patches and the tastiest vegetables you will ever have the pleasure of eating. We can harvest them fresh from the garden beds."

They all agreed, mostly out of curiosity. Even Pickwick jumped about on Jade's palm in rapid leaps. He too enjoyed a feast of fruit and corn pellets. Topaz led the family toward the giant slide, where the stairwell once was. Following in suit, they all sat at the top and slid down towards the lake of water below, feeling the light pelt of sprinklers on the way down. Nearly there, each one inhaled a deep breath. Jade and Micky grabbed hold of their noses. They were ready for the dive.

Reaching the bottom, they all stood up in amazement. They did not sink at all. The water was at least five feet deep. They could see reflections of themselves on the surface. *It was definitely water*, Simon thought as he placed his palm down to explore and was shocked when his hand went through. But, they walked on the surface as though it was glass. How is it that his hand can penetrate it?

Topaz saw his confusion and explained, "your feet are covered with shoes, but your hand is not, and your skin allows certain vibrations to allow the penetration."

Suddenly, a head popped up beside the painting Topaz neared.

"The dolphin!" Jade screeched, looking at Simon with a winning grin.

"Yes, I believe you have met before," said Topaz. "Ernset, I would like you to formally meet the family."

Ernset propped himself up on hind fins and lowered his head in a bow. "It's great to meet you I hope I didn't scare you I was visiting when Medwin closed the gates and was left behind in your world it really is good to meet you I know your names Medwin prophesied your entry now I can go home great to finally meet you are you going into the orchard bring me back some lettuce please I do so miss the seaweed I'll wait here the pond is great…"

Ernset did not cease. He spoke on and on, without allowing a gap for response, not even a breath, jumping from one subject to another, then back to the other. He had a likeable and friendly nature but left one feeling mentally exhausted.

They stood before the picturesque scene showing forests of trees, fields of flowers, and expanses of vegetable gardens. Topaz stepped into the frame looking over her shoulder calling the family to follow.

"Watch your step, though. It can be rather slippery at times."

Simon, Jade and Therese holding Micky followed the possum's advice and carefully stepped over the frame, balancing against the gushing water that was washing their legs. Water from the interior was spilling through the doorway much like a waterfall. The cascading water divided at the base, forming narrow rivers, heading toward the rows of forests and gardens. It was operating like an irrigation system.

Amazing, Therese thought, as they all stood viewing the mass of land surrounding them. Hundreds of acres covered in lush vegetation and home to wildlife including bugs, large and small butterflies, birds, porcupines, and cane toads.

"This way please."
Topaz guided the family toward a swampland of tall reedy grass to the right of the doorway. Large, horned turtles swam over in a line allowing their shells to be used as stepping stones, finishing beside a pair of what looked like cage-top jet skis, each trailed by a cart.

"Hovercrafts, oh and they are cricks," Topaz pointed towards the turtles, answering the puzzled expressions on the faces of Therese, Simon, and Jade. "Well, come along. This orchard is quite enormous; I surely am not walking about. These vehicles work on both land and water."

Topaz leapt into the rear cage of a hovercraft, motioning for Simon to be seated. Therese boarded the other, securing Micky in her rear cage, whilst Jade still cradling Pickwick in her palm, joined Simon, joking about her mother's driving style.

Topaz directed them through the marshy swamp, educating them on the varied plant life and the uses for potions or ailments. Crashing through the tall reeds, they arrived at the opposite end of the swamp revealing forests of fruit trees. The vehicles slowed and began to float in midair, humming softly as both past each row of trees. The trees sprouted fruits of every kind, from the tropical climates, to the cold climates, from all the continents, to all the worlds. There were forests housing the trees from the carnival, growling as the hovercrafts passed, and trees with leaves of pink feathers sprouting coconut-like fruit.

"Pause," Topaz said, and the voice activated hovercrafts came to a halt.
The family had stopped to collect some apples and Topaz showed the plucking technique. Stretching her claw out, she dug her talons into the fruit and pulled.

"Is that it? I thought there was some magical way," Jade whined.

This was not very mystical.

Unlike Topaz, Therese, Jade, and Simon simply grabbed at the fruit then tossed each one into the rear carts and dropped a few. They were startled when the fruit flew back into the cart, tossed by small reptile like creatures, with minor bird heads, leaping rapidly as they collected further droppings.

Micky was quite content for a short period, crunching on his juicy red apple, humming whilst he chewed, when he spotted a cluster of the little creatures. He began throwing samples back and giggled as they scrambled to pick up the fruits.

"Micky, that is quite enough now, you mustn't exhaust them." Topaz smiled she knew he was only playing, but the creatures were becoming agitated. "They are Tefnuts. They maintain the fallen fruit and dispose of the rotten selections."

The possum calmed the creatures and thanked them graciously. They were very helpful indeed.

The family continued to collect more produce; including mandarins, bananas, pears and paw paws. They avoided the unknown varieties for now. They wanted to learn more about the exotic fruits before the taste test and besides, no one was game to pluck from the trees that had whipping branches. Therese was relieved when they moved on and headed for the vegetable gardens.

These gardens had more Tefnuts and were also abundant in various produce, with growths of patches and stalks, from the same continents and worlds. This time the little creatures aided with vegetable selections and tossed the samples into the carts. Micky was too busy looking in another direction and squealed when he spotted a family of lime green butterflies that emerged from within a cabbage; they flew off leaving a trail of pink dust. His squeal hit a higher pitch when he watched a dozen rainbow serpents drinking from a nearby lake. The large reptiles slithered back and forth releasing the intake of water onto crops, like a household garden hose.

The hovercrafts continued onwards, floating towards colourful fields of flowerbeds. Topaz continued the education on handy uses, particularly the mood elixirs that could be made from these crops. There were daffodils, tulips, roses, Venus flytraps, flowers with huge petals, and others that became shy at the attention. It was an abundance of all sorts, including a blue tree that sprouted edible backpacks. Topaz prompted Simon and Therese to pluck one each; they would need them to carry their collection into the house. Topaz also pointed towards a rubber vine adding that the sap acted as disposable gloves and were very handy for the spiked plants.

The family enjoyed the voyage and with much hesitation, agreed to return to the house for a feast. After all, the carts were overflowing, leaving no room for more picking. They returned the hovercrafts to their initial position, climbed back through the door, faced with the eagerly awaiting dolphin.

"Did you bring the lettuce oh thanks you did yum this is the closest thing to seaweed I do like moss too and sometimes eat the tulip leaves," he crunched into the vegetable, "oh yum itsh nishe sho jushy..."

Everyone headed towards the slide in haste, avoiding another endless speech from Ernset, who still managed to talk with his mouth full. Micky fluttered up the slide, while Therese, Simon, and Jade watched as Topaz climbed along the side, using each sprinkler cavity as a foot hold, ascending like a mountain climber. They secured the backpacks full of the fresh produce and followed, laughing as sprinkles of water splashed their faces.

Reaching the top, they braced themselves when the kitchen bench came galloping over, balancing trays and crockery that were leaping on top from the cupboards below. The trays waited impatiently for the platters of fruit and vegetables to be prepared, pushing and shoving each other, vying for the first to hold the food.

All prepared, Therese, Simon, and Micky began devouring the feast. Topaz headed off to the fireplace, discussing the best technique for cooking her beloved apple soup, followed by a pot of water floating carefully, fiddling with its lid, as it caught every drop of spillage.

"Enjoy," Topaz called out, leaving the family to their meal. Cooking the soup was her main focus.

"Come on, Jade, a little bit, okay? How do you know you don't like it if you don't try it?"

Therese was force feeding a fussy Jade, who refused to eat most of the food on the platter before her. Jade's diet consisted of hot chips, macaroni cheese, and noodles. This was not the first time her mother had to use force. It occurred most times, from the time Jade was one year old. Therese won the battle and Jade began the taste test with a screwed expression and sounds to match.

A smile of relief came to Jade's face and she began to enjoy the fruit and vegetables tantalizing her taste buds.

"Yum," she mumbled with a mouthful.

"See, honey girl, try before you judge it." Therese smiled, and then continued her next mouthful whilst Jade shied and smiled at her beloved nickname.

The next hour was not at all serene with the crunching and chomping. Everyone ate until they were full to their toes, then baskets floated across the bench to gather any leftovers and were gone within seconds, heading for the canvas containing the cold room. This acted as a fridge for most foods including some potions.

Simon sank into his seat and rubbed his stomach. He was the first to yawn and the others followed.

"I think we all need to sleep," Therese said as she took charge of the children leading them to her bedroom.

The bedroom had returned to normal with the king size bed, more than enough to accommodate herself, the children and Pickwick. Simon looked about in search of a nap spot when the sofa zoomed over, sliding beneath him and positioned its cushioning to suit Simon's horizontal body. Within moments, all were in deep slumber, with visions of their own powers in their dreams.

They all awoke, refreshed and stretching widely they realised it was time for door two. Jade recalled the location and led the way, but Simon brought them to a standstill.

"Topaz," he hollered, remembering the postponed chat.

A head popped up from the armchair. It was Topaz, yawning with a cackle as she awoke from her nap.

Calling out again, Simon asked, "you said there was more to know. What is it?"

Topaz arose, stretching her back in a curve.

"Ah, yes," she walked toward them. "Therese, the cushion in your room, seated on the chaise. You must take it with you to all gateways. Medwin has prepared potions for many of your needs. Place your arm through the diamond and ask what is required. Now, off you go, gateway two awaits."

"Is that it?" Simon somehow expected more.

"That is all," Topaz added another yawn.

They all shrugged, and then headed for the navy blue door. "Oh, one more thing. I do apologise, Simon. Be sure to fold the cushion and place it where you cannot lose it. Now, that is all."

Simon looked at Topaz with distress, shaking his head. "I think the old possum is getting a bit senile," he whispered.

Therese detoured to collect the cushion, returning to her awaiting family within moments.

"I'm giving it a try," she suggested, as if searching for consent. She passed her hand through the diamond and said, "coffee, please," in hope that a strong, caffeine blend would be supplied to kick start her energy.

She felt a solid object grow in her hand. Pulling her arm back out, she found herself holding a silver mug, filled with a black, tar liquid.

"Not what you expected, eh, mum?" Jade laughed at the look of disgust on her mother's face.

Therese inhaled deeply, she held her nose and sipped the thick brew.

"Yum, it is coffee! At least it tastes like it," she drank more then passed the mug to Simon. It was the best coffee they had ever tasted and, as a joke, Therese suggested, "when this is over, we should open a café. We'll call it The Mud Slush Coffee Shop."

She laughed at her own wit and began to fold the cushion. To her surprise, it folded with ease. The stuffing within seemed to disintegrate for each crease.

Ready for the second door, they stood before it, curious at its pompous character. The door expressed a determined look, with alert eyes and layered bags beneath them.

Speaking to itself, the door was calculating figures and rambling, "at the end of the day we need targets, bottom line is growth, we need more growth," completely ignoring the family as Simon turned the crystal knob. But, it would not open.

The knob glowed and emitted an icy sensation. Simon's hand froze.

"Anti-clockwise," Topaz rattled to Simon, who was rubbing his hand to warm it. "Clockwise will only give you frostbite. Those knobs are carved from elestial crystals found only in the deep arctic."

Simon once again reached out, his hand warming slowly, "like you couldn't have mentioned this before," he grumbled as he opened the gateway.

Chapter 10

THE GAME OF LIFE

The family entered the gateway and fear took hold when the door vanished, leaving no exit point. The path was a giant flat square, with divided panels along the sides. A road began from the section where they stood, bordering along all the edges, with platforms on all the corners. Lined along the roads were rows of trees and light poles that lit each division.

"Gosh, it's, it's a giant mono..." Jade started to say but was interrupted by her mother.

"No way," Therese cut in. "It's definitely a board game but nothing like I've seen before."

They stood on the start platform and looking down, they were taken by surprise, when a pompous voice with a pair of green eyes and a mouth only, said, "You may select a game piece."

Simon scanned the board, "how?" he asked but the face dissolved. "Great! He disappeared. Why doesn't that surprise me? Game piece, what are the pieces?" He searched his thoughts for a moment.

"I know, I know, I bet their similar," Jade was dancing on the spot, as if answering the million-dollar question. "There's a car and..." Before she could say any more, a silver convertible appeared, encasing her into the driver seat. "Cool bananas," she screeched. "I don't even have a license."

Catching on, Simon called out "horse," instantly finding himself sitting in the saddle of a white horse with silver hooves.

Jade prompted Micky to say dog, then a grey, fluffy Maltese terrier appeared with strands of silver fur and began to entertain a laughing and barking Micky who was seated on its back.

"Great," Therese complained. "They're all my favourite pieces. What's left? There's the shoe and..." before she could decide another, the shoe appeared "No! I didn't want the shoe. I was getting to the ship."

"Good idea, mum. Wicks?" Jade prompted Pickwick.

He nodded then squeaked, "Ship."

Pickwick stood on the deck of a silver ship with chiffon sails and misty water floating beneath it, giggling at his new nickname.

"All that ship for a tiny Pickwick," Therese grumbled, as she sat inside a silver tennis shoe that bounced about the platform. "That's not fair."

When the game pieces were ready, the word 'start' embedded on the platform changed to, 'go' and within their hands paper money materialized, totaling two thousand dollars each. They looked up and watched as the large glass orb, filled with numbered ping-pong balls dived toward the centre of the board. It stopped inches from the surface then began to rumble and churn. A funnel appeared, suddenly, two balls shot out and flew towards Jade, both stopped in midair revealing a three and a six. The motor roared, and Jades car moved forward nine spaces. The balls vanished when the vehicle came to a stop.

"What now?" she yelled, asking from a distance.

"I think we go around the board first, before we do anything. Hang tight, squirt," yelled Simon in return as more ping-pong balls shot out, moving his galloping horse forward eleven spaces.

Micky was next, then Therese, each turn came in the same order they had received their game piece. Pickwick was last and had double fours appear on his ping-pong balls, allowing him another turn. His ship floated around the board, past the family, landing on a station, where a steam train billowing smoke tooted its funnel as it parked beside the platform. He had even floated past a diesel freight train, parked at Spencer Street Station, pulling cargo carriages of bricks, timber, and heaped soil.

Passing many sights, they all were bewildered by this world; the board was nothing like the game they knew. It was composed of vacant blocks of land with tufts of grass and weeds. The electricity company had clusters of sparking power poles, and there was an iron slab platform in one corner. The family absorbed their first round of the game in silence with the exception of Micky's barking.

They passed more vacant lands, a parking lot, more train stations, one with a bullet train, the other with a tram, powered by an extended wire clothesline floating above it, and a water field contained an abstract pipe tower, sprouting geyser fountains in all directions. The tree lined streets became more elaborate with landscaping and lawns, more manicured as they neared 'go'.

I guess the more you pay, the better the gardens are, Therese thought.

Simon was the first to pass the go platform and was startled when a bank building appeared, mounting itself to the edge of the board. Paper money floated out of double doors and rested upon his hand.

"I guess, I can buy now," he called out, mainly to keep the others up to date.

Simon had landed on Brisbane road, the vacant block now showed a picketed 'for sale' sign, containing information of purchase price and potential rental return. He counted out the amount needed to purchase the property, then felt the money pull away and watched as it floated through the open bank doors. A scroll titled property deed materialized in his empty hand, showing building costs and more rents. 'For sale', transformed to 'Sold' on the picketed sign, and began to flash with neon lights.

This made Therese eager to buy, but her turn was short, and she still pottered along in the first lap along with Micky and Pickwick. Jade was luckier. Her turn revealed two sets of doubles, this granted her three turns and she passed 'go', landing on 'chance'. A shuffle of cards appeared, dropping one in her lap. Picking it up she read, "Advance forward to Vaucluse."

"Whoo hoo, I'm the best." Jade's convertible sped around the board as the air echoed with her repeated chorus of "I am a champion," stopping on the most expensive stretch of land. "Buy it," she shouted, "Oh Yeah, Oh Yeah, I rule!" The same process occurred, mimicking Simon's experience.

They all continued around the board, buying land, collecting money as they passed the bank and, regretfully, received cards to pay fees on a few occasions. Therese received a card that said, 'pay medical cost seventy-five dollars' and was unaware at first, of the nurse that appeared, holding her hand out, awaiting payment, disappearing the instant she had the money in her possession.

"That was cool," she shouted over to Simon and Jade. "Weird, but cool!"

One experience she did not find cool was landing on 'jail conviction'. The air filled with a howl of sirens; her face paled as she watched two motorbikes screaming toward her then skid to a halt. Two towering police officers leapt from their bikes, pulling her out of the shoe and dragged her across the board to the iron platform.

"Mum, No.o.o! Uncle Simon, do something," Jade screamed in shock, at the sight of her mother being mishandled.

Micky too had been affected, yelling "Bad poo man, leave mama, bad poo man, go way."
The iron floor melted and morphed into prison bars, encasing Therese within the cell. The shoe followed, hopping with all its might to keep up with the officers. Now standing on the outside of the cage, it hopped impatiently, waiting until Therese paid a bail of sixty dollars to be released. The money flew out of her hand, the bars melted down, once again becoming a slab; she was free and ready to continue her play.

The shuffle of cards and experiences were served throughout the game. Simon received fifteen dollars in a 'Miss Glamour Pageant', wiping frantically to remove the makeup that appeared on his face. Jade laughed.
"Mum, did you bring the camera," she called out.

Micky landed on 'GST tax', refusing to part with his money. He played tug of war with a grey suited, spectacled man, who carried a closed briefcase, overloaded with money. The same man reappeared when Jade's card read, 'tax return'. He stood before her, handing over a ten dollar note and attempted to ignore the raspberries that Micky and Pickwick were blowing his way.

Therese received a card saying, 'deceased estate receives two hundred dollars'. A lawyer appeared wearing a silver wig and began to read a will, insisting that she sign a disbursement note when the money was given. Therese had also received a gift certificate of five hundred dollars, to be spent as she desired, for landing on the parking lot platform. Teasing the others, she sang aloud, her version of Jade's song; I am a champion, in her awful opera voice.

Micky however, became disgruntled each time a payment was given to him. He would mumble, "Me want lowwypop, noth wubbith," thinking the notes were paper trash. He became overly excited when his card read, 'Christmas award saver account receive one hundred and twenty dollars'. A Christmas Elf with orange skin, green overalls, and a pointed hat appeared, steering a large sleigh. Micky waited for his presents and lollypop but watched with wide eyes and dropped lip, as the elf disappeared in a jingle of bells. He was only given more paper rubbish, he was not happy!

Pickwick was not a happy camper, either. He had received the 'arrest and convict' card and scurried wildly about the deck of his ship, with an outstretched mouth, squeaking, "Pickwick is cleaning, me is. Goes away, you is bothering me work. Pickwick say, goes away," in his loud voice almost deafening the same officers that arrested Therese.

They chased him all over the deck and Pickwick dodged every attempt at being captured. The challenging run made the two officers sweat and pant to the point of exhaustion. It did not seem to tire Pickwick though; he continued his wiping on the run and made the family laugh tears, as they watched him slide across the surface, using his body as a mop.

Jade stopped her laughter, "Wicks, use your 'free bail card', now!" she recalled the shuffle that was dealt to Pickwick on the second round of their trek. Pickwick responded immediately. He threw the card at the police officers and, in a cloud of dust, both disappeared, sending the ship to visit the iron platform.

The game continued until all vacant blocks were purchased. Simon purchased Sydney, after receiving a double three, and was ecstatic; it was the block he needed to complete his set of scroll deeds. Continuing with the tradition of singing, he bellowed in a deep monotone, I am a champion, emphasizing the 'I'.

"I'm building some houses," he yelled, his excitement apparent. "Let's see... they're a hundred and seventy each. I'll start with two on each," he began to count out the dollars, stopping suddenly, when he heard Jade calling out.

"Look, wow!" she was pointing toward the bank.

Four houses were walking towards Simon, the other two were still advancing from behind the building.

"Wow!" they said simultaneously.

All six houses were different in design. One was a large weatherboard cottage and walked on stilt legs, almost tripping from lack of balance; another was brick veneer with bay windows and a bull nose verandah, maneuvering its concrete slab to walk as though it were made of rubber. There were two with cement rendering, both contemporary yet unique in shape. The other two consisted of a double story shingle home and a timber colonial style dwelling surrounded by a decking. The house lifted up its deck like a skirt and stomped as it walked with concrete stumps.

Finally reaching their destination, the houses parked themselves along the vacant blocks. Driveways and landscaped gardens materialised, including letterboxes labeled with Simon, as the landlord.

"I could get used to this," Simon stated, with a smug look, prompting his horse to leap up on hind legs.

Therese cut in, disturbing his heroic fantasy, "we should swap deeds and get this game over and done with. Remember why we're here?" She thought for a moment. "I think we need to finish, to find the puzzle piece."

She was right; they had been so caught up in the game, enjoying the new experiences, they had forgotten the real purpose of their trip. Everyone agreed and began the swap in order to develop their own sites and bring the game to an end. Calling out their preferred titles, the scrolls floated out of each hand, to the new awaiting landlords.

Jade was delighted with her new deeds, and why not? After all, Vaucluse and Brighton were the exclusive titles. Not wanting any other, she swapped all in hand with Simon and her mother. Micky and Pickwick were not at all interested. In fact, both were on the verge of bankruptcy. Pickwick used his notes as cleaning cloths until they wore to shreds. This prompted Micky to create confetti with his own, that he tossed about the game board, still believing that the money was rubbish.

It was Jades turn and, with a brisk motion, she began fumbling for the amount needed to purchase seven houses. Once again, the structures began advancing from behind the bank; however, this time they were not mere houses, but a variety of huge mansions surrounded by large fences all complete with security monitors flashing, 'Jade Manor'.

"I'm a superstar," Jade whooped. "You call those houses, bah humbug." She laughed at her uncle and continued her turn, rubbing palms together saying, "C'mon, I'm waiting. My mansions are up for rent."

Micky followed next, the ping-pong balls adding to five, moved him directly to Vaucluse.

"Yee ha! Pay me," Jade cheered, but was soon disheartened to find that Micky did not have enough money to cover the rent.

The silver haired dog dissolved beneath him and a magnetic force began to pull him to the start platform. The force sat him on a bench outside the bank and the invisible pressure pinned him in place. Game over for Micky and Jade was thankful to receive his leftover money, even though it was not the total amount owed.

Pickwick's ship was floating near the bank. Micky reached out, wanting desperately to free himself from the bench. Pickwick tore down a sail, throwing one end to Micky in an attempt to tow his new friend on board. But, without success, the force of the magnet held a powerful grip. He was not going anywhere.

Thank goodness! Therese thought, now content that her baby boy was safe from mischief, she turned her focus back to the game. "I'll buy hotels for all my blocks, except for the Tasmania lot. I'll have three houses on each."

Loaded with money, she began sorting the payment, keeping one eye on the bank, curious to see the hotels emerge.

A variety of hotels began stomping their way to their allocated places. There were double storey, three star units, and skyscrapers flashing four and a half stars. Following behind were nine small fibro shacks, ordinary box type dwellings, scrambling to their own position. The hotels stationed themselves, sending minor tremors over the game board. Pools and leisure facilities appeared including billboards, flashing 'Resort Therese', as it played serene music.

"That was awesome," yelled Jade. "We've got to get a game like this one."

Pickwick's turn next landed him on Simon's housing development. He too was out of the game now. His ship melted, and he was sent to wait with a delighted Micky. Simon laughed and galloped forward, his turn landing on his other property.

Landing on Vaucluse once again, Jade had finally collected enough funds to build hotels on her acreage blocks. Her five-star resorts were yet again more spectacular than any other, including surrounding beaches equipped with yachts, floating smorgasbords and boathouse retreats across the estates. What she noticed most of all though, was that unlike the other motels, Vaucluse had open doors leading into the lobby. Calling out, she shared the information, asking what she should do.

"See if you can go in," Simon replied.

Jade tried to leave her car, when a porter rushed over and with a swift motion, he swung the car door open, taking hold of her hand to help her out.

"This way, Madam," he guided her to an awaiting silver limousine.

"Are you checking this out!" Her joyful bellow echoed, as she was escorted into the vehicle.

Therese held her breath, afraid of the unknown. That was her girl, her baby, and she was at a distance, unable to help if something wrong occurred.

The limousine reached the entry marquee and parked. The car door opened and the same porter escorted Jade out of the vehicle. *How did he do that?* she wondered. She had been steered over a bridge and across a long, landscaped driveway. It was not possible for him to get there first. The question was answered almost immediately when she was guided through the front doors, all the staff were identical, wearing the same navy suit and matching fez.

Scanning the foyer, she stopped. There it was! The puzzle piece was resting on the reception counter. She ran back out the entry door and yelled with all her might.

"It's here. The puzzle piece is in here."

She could hear the echo of Simon's voice saying, "great, stay alert okay, we're ready to run, if need be. Get the piece and you run too and please be careful, squirt."

She could also hear the echo of her mother yelling, "I love you, honey girl," a crackle of concern in her voice.

Jade spun her heal and headed back to the counter.

Reaching the counter, she stretched out her arm and touched the puzzle piece. Then with a deep breath and a stomach full of butterflies, she began, "ok, one, two..." on three she grabbed the piece and sprinted out the foyer.

A magnetic force pulled her into the awaiting limousine and it sped off, back in the direction from which it had come. Nothing was happening, no cracks, no tremors, so far so good, her thoughts running faster than the vehicle. The bridge now in sight. It seemed that within moments she was ousted from the vehicle back to where she had begun.

"Not good!" she uttered to herself, in a concerned voice.

Now! she could feel the tremors building, causing her convertible and all the developed sites across the board, to begin the process of dissolving. She could see her mother and Simon racing across the game board on foot toward the start platform. Without a moments haste, Jade also sprinted toward Micky and Pickwick, who watched in fear, now released from the magnetic grip of the bench.

Jade leapt onto the platform in time to see the word 'go' transform to 'game over'. The exit door of the gateway reappeared but gave no comfort, since her mother and uncle had only just passed the midway point, across the board. Jade gripped Micky and Pickwick with force, shaking as she watched the scene before her in horror, not realising that she had dropped the puzzle piece.

The game board lifted at the far end and began folding itself over, closing in on Therese and Simon. A shadow cast across the exit platform like darkened gloom. Jade closed her eyes, tightly hugging her brother and Wicks preparing for the end, when suddenly, she felt a consuming force take hold, crashing them against the exit door. The entry was opened, and the force impelled them through, still holding the firm grip. It was her mother. Therese had made it. They all cried with relief until they realised that Simon was still missing.

Looking out, they saw him slide towards them whilst reaching for the dropped puzzle piece. Thankfully, he had dived in time to seize the piece and slide to safety.

Chapter 11

THE ENCHANTED BATHROOM

Topaz ran towards them, leaping at a far distance, slamming the gateway shut with her body. "Thank goodness," she said. "I am relieved to see you all intact. Medwin does enjoy the worlds of fun and adventure, particularly board games, a child at heart really. I do worry though. Sometimes I feel the element of risk is at a great height. But I had a feeling you would enjoy this gateway."

"WHAT!" snapped Simon. "Enjoy nearly being squashed to death. You can't be serious."

Topaz looked in shock.

"I did," said a shaky voice. Jade gathered her composure and continued her reply, "I had fun, up until the end bit anyway. We played a really fun game and had the chance to play it in a way no one could have thought. I loved it and would play it again. It was unreal." A smug look spread across her face, "and there's another great thing, I WAS THE CHAMPION!" she cheered. "But, next time, I know when to run and why."

Therese embraced Jade, agreeing with her speech and laughing at her winning modesty. Micky and Pickwick joined in the joy then began to squirm hysterically when Therese and Jade started a tickle frenzy. Simon stood near, unable to hold back, releasing a smile, he watched the family roll on the floor.

"I'm sorry," he said and looked at Topaz, "I just don't want anyone to get hurt."

The possum walked over to him, leaping into his arms and planted an affectionate lick to Simon's hand.

"There is no need for an apology, Simon. I am happy to see you care so deeply."

Topaz had previously observed, Simon's love for his family, learning that he would place himself at risk ahead of Therese and the children. It was he who entered each gateway first to make sure the family was safe.

Topaz leapt back to the floor and changed the subject, "is anybody hungry?"

Simon and Therese responded by saying, a snack would be great. Jade and Micky were not interested. They simply wanted to play and roam around the house for a while.

"Ok kids, go for it," Therese said, "just stay close to Micky and keep an eye on him, please, honey girl."

Jade smiled in agreement. There were two reasons for the smile. One was for the nickname and the other because she knew exactly where they were going. She bent down and helped Pickwick scurry up to rest on her palm. Now ready, with Wicks hugging her finger and Micky fluttering close by, the three headed off on their mission.

"Shall we?" Therese and Simon followed the possum to the awaiting dining table and listened intently to the sound of the children. "I thought you might have felt slightly peckish, so I took the liberty and cooked a large broth of apple soup."

Both Simon and Therese hid their disgust, secretly pretending to dry retch when Topaz was not looking.

"There you go, bon appetite," Topaz served bowls full of the mushy liquid with chunks of apple. Then sprinkling clumps of sea salt and a squeeze of lime, she awaited proudly for the taste test.

Looking at each other, as if prompting the other to begin, Therese picked up her spoon, cringing at the first, she opened her mouth.

"Not bad," she swallowed the first mouthful. "Actually, it's really yummy."

Simon followed, both cleaning up the contents in their bowls, finishing with a large burp.

"You are most welcome." Topaz smiled. "A good belch is always a sure sign that you enjoyed your food. And the vinegar sometimes helps with the gases."

Therese covered her ears. She did enjoy the apple soup but had no interest in knowing the ingredients. Some things are best left unsaid.

"Now," Topaz continued, "are you ready for gateway three?"

"Hang on," interrupted Therese. Panic was turning her complexion white, "I can't hear the kids." Jumping up, they all rushed about the house at alarming speed.

Therese stopped suddenly. "I bet you, I know where they are," she hollered and ran towards the artwork containing the general store, not far behind was Simon and Topaz in tow.

She was right! They were there, a chocolate covered Micky, sitting amidst one of the aisles, as Pickwick, frantically scurried about, trying to clean him up. Jade sat on a stool, positioned in front of the lolly counter, creating an art scene using all shapes of the coloured confectionary, sucking on a lollypop. Pickwick struggled to chew a sticky sweet, forcing his mouth open each time it stuck to his jaw.

"Cheeky buggers," Therese laughed, joined by Topaz and Simon at the sight before them. "I think Micky needs a bath before we continue."

Therese headed for the bathroom. Jade and Pickwick followed, curious to see the bathroom and to have a bit of water play with Micky. Simon chose to sit this one out and detoured to the puzzle board, he still clutched the second piece and needed to lay it in place.

Therese and the kids reached the canvas and stepped over the suspended frame. Micky was held by his foot because he was sticky and still covered with remnants of chocolate; Therese thought it best to let him fly to the destination, with a controlled hold, rather than risk being dirtied, herself.

"Oh super, duper cool," Jade screeched when she entered the frame and ran towards the in-ground pool. "This is definitely the best bath I've ever seen." Kneeling down she touched the water, finding the temperature to be perfect.

The bathroom was fantastic! It was a tropical paradise, landscaped with palm trees, organic plants, waterfalls and pebbles surrounding the huge rock pool and spa. Another play pool contained a large central mushroom that sprinkled water and had an assortment of pool toys floating about. Enclosed in huts made of brush fencing were showers and toilets, these stood near a large wave pool mimicking sounds of the ocean. Scattered about the place were hand basins of large shells in a variety of shapes and sizes, some dispensing scented soaps and shampoos.

"Can we pleeeease, have a swim?" Jade begged. Her mother agreed, sending her off to collect swimwear and a change of clothing from the boutique, for each of them. As Jade sped off, Therese began undressing Micky, in preparation for his bath. Concerned about his wings, she was surprised when his shirt came off with ease. His wings had formed into a ghostly mist then returned to solid form, when the clothing was removed.

Returning in a flash, Jade placed the clothing on a bamboo sun lounge, once again racing off to an enclosed change room, her mother close behind, entering the hut beside her. Very soon, everyone was dressed in swimwear and ready for the swim.

Jade crouched in midair then dropped like a water bomb into the wave pool creating a big splash. Pickwick followed her and dived with a tiny plop, hardly enough to make a difference to the water surface at all. Therese and Micky chose the play pool. It was shallow, and the mushroom could be used as a shower.

"Hey stop it!" Jade shouted and looked over to Micky. But her brother was not the one tossing pebbles into the pool.

A tiny person only about three inches high with a squashed face, as though it had been run over was standing on the sand surrounding the pool, tapping his foot, waiting for a reaction.

"Well, come on, Missy, you're supposed to dive to the bottom and collect the stones. Medwin loves playing this game," he said in a tiny gruff voice as she floated with the waves, staring with curiosity.

"Who and what are you!" Jade was surprised then noticed others creeping out from shafts within the rocks, all with the same distorted little faces.

"I'm Frigg and we are Coblies. Pleased to meet you, Miss. Sorry I startled you. I just thought you wanted to play."

Jade swam closer, with Pickwick struggling to keep up.

"It's nice to meet you, too. But what are you doing? Do you live here, all of you?" she watched the assortment of Coblies abseil to where Frigg stood.

"That is surely a yes, Miss. We Coblies are the caretakers of these gardens and we carve the rock pools. Medwin was kind enough to let us live here when our world was destroyed by those evil Sylphs. Our cousins the Drydads are over there," he pointed to a cluster of palm trees. "They seed the plants and help them grow."

Jade turned her attention to the tiny green sprites with human features and floppy ears, sliding down the tree trunks. She waved as they saluted in greeting.

"Wow, it's nice to meet all of you and I think this place rocks. I love it. You've all done a really good job." She bellowed to her mother, introducing her new friends.

Therese took hold of Micky and joined Jade and Pickwick in the large pool. They all had fun playing the pebble game, whilst eight Drydads held Micky afloat in the water. The drenched Drydads were not overly pleased with Micky's splashing.

A couple of hours had passed, and Therese insisted they finish, "come on, time to get out. Your uncle and Topaz are probably wondering what's taking us so long."

They all hopped out, to Jade's dismay. She could not wait for her next bath.

Reaching for a towel that was supplied by a helpful trolley, Therese and Jade stopped and watched in amazement as the water from both pools evaporated; then, within seconds, both refilled. They were now dressed in dry clothes, chosen by Jade. Therese shook her head at the selection. Camo prints for all of them. "Typical," she said and embraced Jade, playfully rubbing a fist on her head.

Everyone called out parting words and a big thank you to their new pool mates then headed toward the exit with Pickwick still shaking off his water-soaked fur. This made his body look almost like the size of a marble and his limbs like gangling spaghetti. Stepping through the frame, they felt a gush of hot air blow dry any remaining residue of water.

"That was the coolest," Jade said.

"You've said that about most places, you dag!" Therese hugged her daughter, and both laughed as they headed to reunite with Simon and Topaz. Micky fluttered off in front of them while Pickwick scurried behind, now a ball of fluff.

Simon and Topaz could hear the approaching voices of Therese and the children. "In here guys. Sounds like they've had a lot of fun," Simon continued his conversation with Topaz, as the echoing laughter neared.

Both had spent their time in deep discussion, prompting Simon to mention the dream he had experienced during the previous nap. Topaz gave counsel, explaining the reason why, Simon, Therese, and both children would continue having those particular dreams. The dreams were a source to help boost their inner abilities, enabling them to unlock and understand their gifted powers. Topaz also explained that Medwin had gone to all lengths, creating obstructions, should Mulgot and Rosmer, manage to obtain any of the five items. The discussion carried on, as the family approached.

Simon looked toward Therese, laughing as he joked, "nice threads, sis. A Jade selection, I presume. Very cute, you all coordinate."

Therese joined in laughing, feeling as though they were about to embark on a military mission. Simon stopped, then with a serious tone, explained his dream once again, discovering that both Jade and Therese had experienced the same sort of dream during their nap. Asking them to take a seat, he and Topaz repeated their previous chat.

"So when I saw myself in different colours and patterns this was part of the boost," Therese disclosed her dream. "I looked pretty freaky sometimes, I think I prefer to crush boulders and carry canons like your dream Simon."

"I reckon my dream was cool," Jade smiled, recalling her dream. "I had yellow ooze and purple dust come out of my hands. It was really mucky and tingled at the same time." She waved her hands about pretending the ooze was pouring out.

Topaz ignored Jades clowning around then said. "There is no need to worry Therese, however you appear it is not permanent, but it will be a great asset for your treks. The dreams will continue, some may not make sense but they all have an important message and will prompt your abilities."

All up to date with the information, Jade was the first to say, "Can we go now? I can't wait to see what's behind door three."

Simon had entered the general store earlier and found a child harness. He secured it around Micky's waist and stretched the lead, this would definitely stop his little nephew from taking off and still give him the chance to flutter about. Now they were ready and began the walk towards the gateway.

Therese stopped for a moment to pat the leg pocket of her camo pants, making sure the folded cushion was still in it. She had forgotten to remove it from her other clothes, and was relieved when the trolley shook it out, reminding her to collect it. Jade chatted with her uncle as they approached the next gateway, describing all aspects of the bathroom, adding that bath time was definitely fun time now, she then stopped.

"It looks sad," she said showing concern when they stood before the pale blue door. "What's the matter? Are you ok?"

The door opened its mouth to answer, then sighed, as it closed again feeling too bored to respond. It began to pucker and then puffed its cheeks out, releasing them, repeating the process, attempting to cure its humdrum feeling without much success. Not stopping, the door watched with droopy eyes, as the family turned the knob and entered the gateway.

Chapter 12

THE SILENT MOVIES

This world was dark and other than the light from the doorway, it was difficult to see their surroundings. A bright headlight appeared then approached quite rapidly, the family braced themselves for what was coming.

Phew! Simon thought and exhaled a relaxed deep breath when they saw a dark-skinned valet, wearing a white suit, closing in. He held a torch, aiming the light directly at the exit and in complete silence he began to mime an action, asking them to close the door.

"Oh, sorry," replied Simon, pushing the door shut. "I forgot again."

Before Simon could ask a question, the valet raised his hand as a stop sign, holding his other hand up, he fanned out a deck of cards. The valet handed a piece of the blank cardboard to each family member including Pickwick. Then stretching out his arm with an open palm, he pointed left of the doorway, indicating the direction they must go. Bowing his head, he began walking backwards, fading in an instant.

The round metal surface they stood upon began to rotate slowly, releasing a path that coiled out at one edge point, into the distance. The lights dimmed, and a row of arrowed fairy lights highlighted their way.

"The card, mum," Jade spoke in excitement as writing began to appear. "It's a movie pass. Admit one only," she read aloud. "Cool, I hope it's a good one, like a comedy or something, and not a boring, girly, love story."
Therese rolled her eyes at Jade's comment; comedies were great but there was nothing wrong with girly, chick flicks.

"Well, I hope it's an action movie with fast cars and pumping music," added Simon.
This time, both Therese and Jade rolled their eyes, laughing at his driving performance. Micky and Pickwick joined in making vroom sounds.

"Boys will be boys." Therese smiled. "Come on, let's go, or would you three, prefer to play cars for awhile?"

Tracking the row of lights, the family embarked onwards, toward the next part of the gateway and realised, as the edge became closer, that the rotating surface, on which they walked was a giant, encased movie reel. The movement ceased and the now uncoiled path formed a stairway leading from the edge of the film case, down to a base where a thick grey curtain, blocked their way. The dull velvet fabric also hid the remainder of the path.

Simon led the walk down and handed the lead that secured Micky, over to Therese. Studying the path before taking his foot off the last step, Simon's excitement began to show.

"Wow, this path is the negative strip for a movie. This is fantastic."
Bracing himself, he stepped forward with one foot only, balancing on the other leg, as the curtain began dividing across like a folding wave, revealing the world hidden behind it.

"Gosh," yelped Therese, "we're in a black and white movie. Great! Now we're back to bland. Boy, does this place need some colour!" She was not too disappointed, though. In fact, she was in complete awe, watching her surroundings.

There was commotion and scenes happening in all directions, but there was no sound.

An odd-looking fellow wearing a tail suit, waddled about and scratched his head, a group of children played hopscotch, others played jacks, some were licking ice creams and a couple ran about, getting into all kinds of mischief.

Men and women dressed in old fashioned clothing rode about on penny farthings, while others stood beside each other, rapidly blinking their eyes, some of the women, dropping handkerchiefs on purpose. A wind-up car full of policemen wearing tall hats, chased a man wearing an eye mask. There was also a seedy looking character with a long, curled moustache, wearing a top hat, running in many directions, as he carried a lady, who fought to be released and another woman, tied to a railway track fought to free the ropes, as a train approached.

The lack of noise was surreal, in particular the fire engine that was steered about in fast motion with a firefighter holding a thick hose, watering everything in sight. It would surely be loud with its clanging and flashing lights, not to mention all the rest of the utter mayhem. This gateway was a madhouse and not one of these characters, seemed to notice the presence of the family.

"Is this what you and Uncle Simon used to watch, mum?" Jade asked. "You know, back in the dark ages when you were a kid? It's pretty boring!" she smiled in a cheeky way.

"Oh, ha, ha, you're so funny. I'm not that old, you little monkey," Therese leered playfully at her daughter's head, "but I have watched some of Nan and Pops old silent movies."

"Me too," Simon replied with sarcasm, "back when we walked a million miles to school without shoes, fighting off the dinosaurs." They all laughed now at the silly conversation.

Simon's laugh caused him to lose balance, edging him forward onto the path, his foot touched the photo, centered on the negative strip.
"Oh, noooo…" Simon's voice echoed, as his foot was sucked through the negative, the force also pulling the rest of his torso.

Therese and Jade screamed in horror. They froze in shock, still standing upon the steps.

"Wha... what now, mum?" Jades mouth was still gaped.

Therese shook her head, not knowing what to do or what just happened.

Simon landed on the ground inside the negative, his distorted body from the suction returned back to normal. Looking down, he watched as the movie pass disintegrated in his hand. Looking up he saw the smoked glass window, which had absorbed him, hearing the echo of Jade speaking above. *What now?* he wondered.

Simon focused his attention on the surroundings.

The set was constructed to look like an unkempt, lounge room and he could see a slapstick comedy being acted out before him. It was a scene of three men with bobbed hair trimmed above their ears, knocking each other across the head and flicking each other's ties. One kept tripping over even when there was no obstacle, and another ran on the spot, because he was held by the belt of his pants. They stopped after a few moments and looked directly at Simon.

"You can see me?" he asked in surprise.

The trio nodded and began to approach, recommencing their antics with each other.

"I'm looking for a puzzle piece, can you help? And can you also tell me how I get out of here." Simon inhaled a deep breath and waited for the answers.

Not one man spoke, they mimed just as the valet had, beginning with a frustrating game of charades.

They played two games containing more slapstick antics. Each time Simon guessed wrong, the man acting it out was knocked in the head and pushed away. Another would take a turn, thinking he was the better mime and was pushed aside by the other. It was just as crazy as the madhouse above.

After what seemed like hours of charades, Simon finally discovered, in game one, that the puzzle piece was inside a negative along the path. Game two revealed the way to exit was to repeat the words, 'End of movie'. Without wasting a moment longer, Simon spoke the words and felt himself being pulled back up through the window, his body distorting once again. The three comedians waved a goodbye, still carrying on the antics by sidestepping in front of each other, wanting to be the first to wave.

Feeling his body return to normal, Simon was relieved to be back on the path and to see his awaiting family.

"Thank goodness, that's over," he said. "Have you guys been standing there all this time, it's been hours?"

Therese and Jade looked at each other, assuming Simon was in a state of shock.

"Are you okay?" Therese asked, Simon responded with a yes and continued the account of his experience and information.

"At least now we know where to look and to be very choosy because there's only four tickets left." Simon turned his focus to the path, gasping at the sight. The path was at least a mile long containing multiples of negatives. Four tickets only and hundreds of negatives, this was not as easy as he thought.

"By the way, just so you know, we've only been waiting a few seconds. Are you sure you're alright?" Therese was still concerned.

Simon assured his sister but was surprised by the statement. *Very odd,* he thought, *but who knows what to expect.* Beginning their journey once again and tight rope walking along the edge of the path, all were cautious and avoided touching the pictures within the frames, until they were ready to enter.

"Where should we start?" Jade asked.

Simon and Therese were leaning over each scene hoping to see the puzzle piece.

"I can't see it in any of these,' said Therese, she was feeling overwhelmed.
Simon walk ahead to look through more.

"What luck!" he called out, pointing to a row of negatives from a short distance. "These have 'Theatre closed' written on top." He stepped on one, "and we can walk on them. Those over there say, 'Under construction'. I bet we can walk on those too." He stepped on the others. "At least that eliminates some of the search."

Jade walked over, placing Pickwick down. They both began dancing on the closed negatives. Micky started his own jig, fluttering as far as the lead would extend. He also giggled, as he watched the mayhem in the sidelines, particularly the fire engine zooming around, soaking the sights.

"You know, mum. This gateway is pretty fun," Jade was also watching the chaotic scene. "The people act weird and dress silly. They're all nuts and I reckon they're funny. Maybe I'll watch Nan and Pops movies one day."

Therese was distracted. She was leaning over a negative and finally after many searches she spotted the hidden puzzle piece. Taking in a deep breath, she stepped onto the surface. The force sucked her through, like a powerful vacuum cleaner.

The set was the exterior of a bakery with a little orphan boy standing alone, his face pressed against the window. A chubby man wearing an apron ran out the door forcing the boy to move away from his bakery. Therese stood there and watched, tears cornered her eyes. She wanted to take this boy home, so he could escape the nasty man! Another person walked out of the bakery and gave a loaf of bread to the little child. The boy was thankful and skipped off, biting chunks off the loaf. Therese continued watching, suddenly hearing the echoed voices of Simon and Jade calling.

"Have you got it?"

She shook her head and muttered, "Remember what you're here for."

Looking around she saw the cart full of various shapes. This was what she had assumed to be puzzle piece, but she was wrong, it was only empty and torn boxes. Repeating the words to exit, she returned to her family.

It was Jade's turn.

Entering the scene, she found herself amidst the set of a candy store. "Whoo hoo, I picked the best one," she cheered.

Pickwick followed, wanting to be with her all the time.

"Noooo..." she could hear Simon yelling from above. "That's a waste of a movie pass." Too late, the ticket was gone.

Jade reached for a lolly, wanting to try it, even though it was grey.

"Yuk!' she spat it out the instant her taste buds kicked in. "Wicks don't eat any of this stuff. It tastes off."

Jade wiped her tongue with her sleeve and walked over to a poster, she was disappointed to find it was not the puzzle piece, only a torn-up sign, missing all the edges. They both said, 'End of Movie' and returned to an irate, Simon.

"Wicks, we needed that movie pass," he scowled.

"Pickwick is sorry, me is Mr. Simon. Me just wanted me Jade," he squeaked his apology then scurried up Simon's body, onto his face then hugged his nose with affection. Feeling his heart melt, Simon mellowed and gave Pickwick a gentle pat. Pickwick scurried back to Jade and the family continued the search, looking above the negatives.

Micky was the only one left holding a movie pass. Therese was worried, and she began to panic at the thought of her baby entering a negative alone. Simon coaxed Micky into handing over his pass, hoping to use it himself. The plan did not work.

Simon held the pass for a moment, but it flew out of his hand and back to the original bearer. Micky giggled, thinking it was a game of catch wanting to play again. After a few attempts, Simon decided to take some drastic action.

"I'll gate crash and see what happens. Any thing's worth a try." Simon jumped through the nearest negative and felt the force of large arms grab hold, tossing him back out. "Great! Magical bouncers," he complained. "They threw me out. But, I was able to glimpse the set. I'm jumping back in and I'll check the place out quickly."

Therese joined in the search, tying the end of Micky's lead to a cavity along the edge of the path. Both began leaping into individual scenes, feeling the force toss them out like rag dolls.

Trying to control her balance, from the toss, Therese was shouting with excitement, "It's here, it's in here," she pointed.

Simon untied Micky and ran to the scene housing the much-awaited puzzle piece. Jade and Pickwick stood beside Therese, both jumped with joy and sang 'you are the champion' with their loudest voices. Therese stopped silent, once again, panic overcame her, remembering that Micky was the only ticket holder, therefore he was the only one who could enter.

"It's okay, mum. Micky will be fine," Jade hugged her mother. "We'll call out to him and help." Pickwick also scurried to aid in comfort and hugged her finger.

Simon began explaining the task ahead as Micky giggled. "Ok, I ave lowwypop," he said because his uncle promised to give him a lollypop when they returned to the house. Therese and Jade closed in with a tight embrace, almost suffocating Micky with squeezes and kisses.

"Ok, bub, you go down and get the paper on the table. I love you." Paper was the best way she could describe it. Therese felt her heart beating rapidly she was flooded with concern.

Micky flew to the negative and landed with his feet down he entered.

The set consisted of tables only. Each table had an item on it, there was a cup on one, another had a plate and another had a bowl, all with a piece of dinnerware, the odd one out had the puzzle piece.

Micky fluttered about the tables picking up items calling out, "dis one, um, dis one."

It was a slow process, but he finally picked up the puzzle piece and everyone called out, "yes".

"Now say 'End of Movie'," Therese repeated the exit words, over and over again, until Micky finally copied her sentence. "Thank goodness," she sighed with relief, now holding her baby boy, kissing his cheeks and forehead like a woodpecker.

Removing the puzzle piece from his grip, she suddenly felt the path move beneath their feet. The negative strip was winding itself back into the reel case. Looking behind them, they saw the end of the path nearing, with no way past but down.

"Run!" Simon shouted grabbing hold of Jade's arm.

Therese clutched Micky and they all broke into a sprint.

The path shortened and began to spool faster into the case, aiding their evacuation. But, it began to wiggle and jerk making the surface unstable, the family struggled to keep balance.

Simon, Jade, and Therese neared their destination and prepared to ascend the stairway, regretfully finding that the steps had disappeared. Thinking quickly, Simon gently tossed Jade onto the platform, boosted Therese and Micky then pulled himself up to safety.

They stood on the metal case and continued the sprint to the exit door, following the rotation of the surface. Now inches from the door, they could feel a rocking movement below their feet. The film had completely reeled in and the case began descending. Simon grasped the handle and holding on he opened the door. He reached over and scooped Jade with his free arm, guiding her through the exit. Then catching Therese by the arm, he released Micky from his mother's grip. Micky was elated with his freedom, he fluttered up and through the doorway to safety.

Therese and Simon looked below, dangling in midair, watching as the case collapsed, down into a black hole. Simon pulled his sister up, then swung her through the opening, still clutching the puzzle piece in her other arm. Therese jumped up instantly and reached over, grasping the opposite knob. She towed the door closer and helped her brother climb into the house.

Stretching, Simon stood up and closed the gateway, "that was fun," he rubbed his palms together. "Bring on the next world."

They all laughed, echoes filled the house when Topaz ran into the room with a pleased expression.

"Ah, lovely too see you all. I trust you found the gateway enjoyable, judging by the merriment."

"It was fantastic," replied Therese. "Bizarre, but fun. The collapse wasn't as bad as the others. At least that's what I think," she tucked in her shirt, "maybe because we expect it now, so we prepare ourselves and seem to have more control, especially my big, strong brother."

Simon laughed and flushed slightly at the compliment. "Thanks, sis. You did pretty good yourself. You too, squirt," he reached over and embraced Jade then gently patted Pickwick.

"By the way," Topaz said, "if you are looking for Micky, I would check the candy corner."
They all looked directly at Topaz, noticing a smudge of chocolate on her face and body.

"And in case you are wondering, I followed Micky into the general store to watch him. As you can see, he force fed me chocolate." Topaz finished, with a disgruntled expression.
The family erupted with laughter.

Chapter 13

A GUESS CAN BE DEADLY

Therese handed the puzzle piece to Simon asking him to lay it in place and darted off immediately to collect her son. She envisioned a chocolate covered Micky, fluttering about in hypo mode from sugar overload. Jade and Pickwick followed close behind, not wanting to miss any opportunity to visit the candy store.

Stepping over the frame, Therese found Micky quite clean, seated on the candy counter, with chocolate stained hands only, dribbling as he sucked on three lollypops at once.

"Mama," he muffled, "pulling out the triple treat, "me ave lowwypop."

Therese and Jade laughed at the sight; after all, Simon had promised him one.

"Wow, so you have, bub. You're a lucky boy," his mother replied.

Jade helped herself to a handful of confectionery and a few lollypops, whilst Pickwick scurried over to Micky, frantically wiping his dirty hands and sticky face.

"Come on, you lot. It's time for the next gateway."

Therese embraced her son and they headed back to Simon, all sucking on lollypops, speaking in muffled voices.

"Aww, where's mine?" Simon pretended to be disappointed.

Jade reached into her bulging pocket and handed over a sweet, she offered another to Topaz, who politely refused.

"Mmmm, sugar energy, just what we need for the next task." Simon unwrapped his sweet and wasted no time for the taste test.

Everyone was mumbling now as they enjoyed their candy.

"Oh, what a glamorous sight you all are," Topaz said sarcastically. "May I say, good luck with gateway four and enjoy the sugar rush on your journey." She laughed with a rattle and watched as the family headed for the next adventure.

"I think it's this one," Simon turned the knob.

"No. Unc—" Jade was unable to finish her warning. Simon pushed the door open.

It was the wrong door.

"Oh nooo!" Simon screamed.

A blast of psychedelic colour hurled the family backwards. Simon was injured. Touching his face, he felt a gaping wound on his cheek, oozing a dull black slime.

Topaz leapt from the distance and slammed the door shut, with extreme force. They all looked stunned, but with luck and the shield of Simon's torso, no one else was hurt.

"Wrong door. That was not gateway four," snapped Topaz in a high-pitched scowl.

Simon began to breathe rapidly in a panic, the slimy ooze began gushing and the wound was growing by the second.

"Jade, quickly, you must apply your power, now!" Topaz shouted.

"But," Jade was about to ask how, when Topaz interrupted.

"Haste is needed, touch a gem on your choker and place your other hand on the wound. Then you must focus, picture the healing wound within your mind." The possum was anxious her nerves a mess.

Jade placed a fumbling finger on the stone then reaching over she placed her other hand on the wound, cringing as the tar like substance covered her arm, it was ice cold and felt as though it was drawing blood through the pores on her skin.

Nothing occurred; the wound opened further, sinking Jades hand and began spouting a stronger gush of slime.

"Quickly, try another gem," Topaz was now hysterical.

Moving her index finger to the centre stone, Jade focused, picturing an image of Simon's face as it was before the injury. The fountain of slime ceased, and the wound faded before their eyes.

"Oh, thank goodness," Topaz sighed, still shaking from the experience. "The wound would have continued to expand until it encompassed Simon's entire body, leaving not even a shell. Now please concentrate. Gateway four is where?"

With a series of deep breaths, they all calmed their shock.

"I know now," Jade was observing her arm with fascination, as the slime faded. Then with a blissful tone she said, "I felt it. I could feel the magic. It was like the tingle you get from pins and needles, only it was warm." Looking up she continued, "I know how to heal now, I remembered my dream. It showed me how to concentrate. Oh, and I know where door four is too," a wide grin spread across her face. "It's the inside of the front door, downstairs."

Fortunately for the family, Jade's memory worked quite well. Simon found the number system a little odd. "You'd think it would be upstairs, near door three," he said. "Why spread them like this?"

Topaz thought for a moment. "Medwin enchanted these gateways in abstract order to confuse. However, the order of his system has meaning. Unfortunately though, I do not recall the reasoning, but I now remember what happens when you enter in the wrong order due to that horrific incident. I am sorry Simon."

Topaz bowed her head with shame, a sense of guilt entering her thoughts. Her absent-minded ways were not always comical, it also put the family at risk.

Simon rolled his eyes. Unfortunately for the family, Topaz was an ancient and vague possum that did not have a memory like Jade. He could see the sorrow in her expression and quietly complained when he followed the family down the water slide.

"Weeeeee," echoed Micky's voice, as they slid to the lower level.

Chapter 14

PREHISTORIC WATERS

Standing up, they headed towards the next gateway. Simon stopped; his thoughts went back to what Topaz had said. He wanted to test the theory of bare skin penetrating the glass-like water, so he removed his footwear and rolled up his baggy pants. His feet sunk instantly, the water reaching his kneecaps. *Nice* he thought the water felt warm and soothing. He reached back down and placed his shoes back on meanwhile Therese and Jade waited impatiently, eager to enter the next venture.

Door four was unlike the previous ones. It contained no face, only puckered mouths blowing bubbles and the background was a panel of flowing water that felt solid to touch. Simon turned the handle and scanned the area first, informing the family that it was safe. They entered, and Simon began to close the door when he felt an impact. Ernset came crashing through the entry, nearly barreling him over.

"Oh I'm so sorry really I am are you ok are you sure your okay I just wanted to go home this is the way to my world I can show you the way you can meet my family really are you sure you're alright I'm so so sorry..." Ernset mouthed his usual continuous, rapid speech as he closed the door, dusting Simon off in his attempt to apologise.

They stood on the water, which reflected like glass surrounded by a long-arched tunnel with walls made only of water. But, the walls were not solid like the ground; some force was holding it back. Rotating their heads, they watched in awe as an array of sea life swam about the opposite side, thankfully, the creatures could not break through the protective barrier, some tried nevertheless.

Jade walked over to the wall and was surprised when her hand penetrated the surface. She moved quickly, jerking her arm back when something swam close and aimed for her hand with its jaws. The creature crashed against the barrier.

"Wow!" she exclaimed and was a bit shaken. "It's that sea serpent from the carnival."

Pointing, she began to count others, exclaiming wow! when she spotted double headed ones and others with dragon like heads.

She stopped, with her finger in midair, turning to her mother she asked, "what's that, and that, and those?" Therese watched, unable to answer.

There was common marine life Jade could name including the giant axolotls and seahorses, but the other unusual sea animals of various shapes and sizes looked like prehistoric creatures she had only seen in history books. Many had defined sharp teeth, long tentacles, and antennae. Some had paddle shaped snouts and large lobed fins. Others were four-legged dragon-like lizards and some were translucent, revealing their skeletal structure.

Ernset was happy to be the teacher he began the lesson.

"They are splitfins those are fluke tails those ones are stumptooth minnows the see-through ones are shiners those paddle snouts are toadlets my favourites are the pupfish near that coral…"

The marine lesson continued, this time the family had an interest in what Ernset said, even though he went on and on. They proceeded the walk through the tunnel with echoes of awes, as they spied and learned of the new forms of sea life.

Jade watched Ernset for moments, needing her curiosity answered. "How come you can walk on your fins, especially when you're not in water?"

"Not just me," he replied, "we all can we just avoid it now because it's more fun to swim back in the prehistoric days all the sea animals walked on the dry land from the whales to the smaller fish but those land animals always hogged the best parts and feeding spots so we thought we'd claim the seas as our own its nicer anyway with a better food supply boy did they lose out…"

Jade interrupted again, before Ernset could continue. "So, do you guys have a king or something, like Neptune?"

He stopped for a moment as if lost for words. "What is it with you humans and fairytales is your head full of clam shells do you really think a half human would rule the seas no way get with the seaweed bro our king is the only rightful ruler he is ancient he is intelligent he is generous he …"

"Then who is it?" she asked impatiently.

"You'll see you'll need to meet him to get that puzzle piece he is all mighty he is caring he knows all he..." Ernset replied not answering the question and continued with his long-winded speech yet again.

The family placed their hands over their ears to block the echoes of his infatuation with his king. *Don't ask Ernset too many questions*, they all thought simultaneously, making a mental note in their minds.

Approaching the end of the tunnel they watched as Ernset ran ahead stepping through the wall.

"C'mon I can't wait mum and dad are gonna love you do you like seaweed and coral oh yum golly I've missed it hurry follow me."

They could hear no other word as he disappeared behind the wall.

Simon entered first. It was another wall of water, but he felt dry and warm as he passed through it. The family followed, and all were surprised to find themselves standing on the ocean floor, still feeling dry and warm, with the ability to breathe with ease. Ahead they saw a range of dolphins swimming towards Ernset, calling out welcomes and words of relief.

The female tossed her body on him, pecking and repeating, "My baby, oh my dolphy, I missed you, are you okay?"

Ernset answered in a shy voice, "Yes mum I'm fine I've had plenty to eat Topaz gave me food from the orchards oh hang on Mum Dad and you bunch of clam heads," he looked over to the group of his brothers and sisters, then continued in a more excited tone, "this is Therese Simon Jade Micky and Pickwick the ones Medwin talked about and..."

The dolphins squealed in happiness, halting the speech Ernset was ready for, obviously knowing how much he could ramble. They swam over, and each dolphin pecked and pampered the family members. Micky returned that favour with head butts.

"Where're my manners?" Ernset's mother stopped the commotion, "I'm Florian, this is Lister my husband and this lot is our other children, Yanto, Garm, Balder, Bor, Freya, Venter, Gazelle, and Gillicus. Come along dears, I'll prepare a nibble. You must be famished."

Following, the family tested the water by walking, running, jumping, swimming and Jade's favourite, doing a series of somersaults. They reached a structure of tall, bright pink coral with matted vines of tiny white lilies, and large cavities about the façade.

"Welcome home fish face," Florian said and gave her son a peck, this was obviously a compliment because of the smirk on his face. "Now, Therese, you and the children can take a seat over there, on those sea sponges. Simon, you can help Lister carry out the shells. I prepared some nibbles earlier this morning."

Simon, Lister, and a tribe of smaller dolphins returned carrying oyster shells and clam shells containing an assortment of sea vegetation.

"Yum, um, num...," the dolphin family dived into their feast, devouring the mix of salad compositions and coral they broke apart like bread. Micky hand fed the smaller dolphins, missing their mouth on most attempts as Pickwick frantically cleaned the mess.

"Dive in."

Therese could hear the offer of food before her, reaching over she scooped a handful of the salad containing slimy seaweed, lilies, moss and cactus plants. Placing it in her mouth and holding back the lump in her throat, she chewed then swallowed, feeling her stomach begin to churn. Ernset noticed and broke into a chuckle at the seasick look on Therese's face.

"You humans just can't stomach good food," he said still laughing.

Simon and Jade watched in disgust, both refused politely as the food was offered to them, thankfully it was disappearing fast.

Content and full to their fins, the dolphin family floated above their seats as they burped bubbles. The smaller dolphins yawned then headed to the coral home and entered through the cavities, preparing for sleep. Therese sighed with relief. There were no leftovers, this left no more offers for a taste test.

Ernset rubbed his belly with his flipper and asked, "Do you want a kip, or would you prefer to see the king the fair and good king the great…"

Cutting in before Ernset could continue, Simon replied, "I think we'll see the king, just get the puzzle piece and go home. Thanks for the offer, though."

With that, everyone said their goodbyes. Florian pecked the family once again, wishing them luck and ordered her son to return home also demanding he get up to no other shenanigans. Ernset led the way, complaining about his mother treating him like a calf when he was interrupted by a screech.

Micky squealed with laughter. He felt the impact of a small dolphin crash at his feet. It was Gillicus. The small dolphin had raced to catch up to the family, not realising how close he was because his eyes were shut to avoid the water pressure from the speed.

"Gilli you clam butt go home," Ernset bellowed to his little brother.

"Don't call me names Ern, I'll tell ma, and if you don't let me come, I'll be sure to tell ma."

Ernset grumbled his agreement, ordering his brother to behave, "but you have to stay close alright! I don't want ma to swim down on me if you get gobbled up by a fomorian."

Answering the family's puzzled expression, he explained, that the fomorians were savage demons of the sea, hiding in the darkest cavities waiting for their prey; they were black, two legged reptiles with four arms and razor sharp claws. Though fomorians were blind, they could sense the vibrations of an approaching victim and shred them to pieces before devouring them.

The family swam through the ocean, their bodies light and the scenery blissful. They even met a parade of Ernset's friends. Forsetti, a stump tooth minnow, with a flat face, spat bubbles as he greeted them through his chunk of a tooth. His round belly and wart infested yellow scales quivered when he spoke. Another was a grey minke whale named Gazelle, she too was obsessed with the king saying he was her hero and portraying him as the all mighty wolf of the sea.

A large serpent, Gopa, rushed to the family, wrapped himself around Therese, and welcomed her to the waters; Ernset could see the panic and forced Gopa to release his grip. Later, he explained that the myths were not true. Serpents were simply quite affectionate. The sharks were quite friendly too, but it was difficult to warm to some of the prehistoric fish. The family found their large, sharp teeth quite intimidating and the slimy bodies covered in warts, disgusting.

Relived to swim on the family resumed the trek. Micky and Gillicus played tag, venturing off in their chase whilst Ernset continuously berated both boys.
"I'll donk both you clam heads if you don't stay close," he yelled.

The dive continued as they swam through coral, over rocks and sea plants avoiding any dark caves or bushes. Simon was convinced he glimpsed a Fomorian snatch a glider with its talons, disappearing into the thick growth of seaweed vines.

"Look," Jade called out, "is that, a mermaid?" Everyone looked, just in time to see the tiny half human, half salmon darting off, disappearing within a cluster of coral.

"No," Ernset looked about with rocket speed. "That was a seasibyl she comes from the family of merfolk and if you catch one she'll grant you three wishes and," he stopped, darting off to chase another seasibyl, heading in the same direction as the other one had. She swam with all her might, dodging and spinning in all directions, heading straight for Jade.

With one quick swoop Jade shouted, "I got her, whoo hoo," singing, "I've got three wishes."
She felt a warm sensation in her hand and her palm opened slowly like a flower petal. Resting before her was a blonde seasibyl, with a pretty face, violet eyes, and pink tail, calming her breath from the chase.
She floated to Jade's eye level and said, "my name is Amiya. Is there a wish, you would like me to grant?"

Ernset swan closer to Jade, "the king wish for the kingdom to come to us it saves us looking for him."
Jade spoke her wish and Amiya vanished immediately after reciting the words for the charm. Jade was disappointed.
"Don't worry," said Ernset, "you still have two more you just say her name and ask the wish and it will be granted by the binding law of the sea."

Suddenly the sand began to churn on the sea bed. Plants shook and currents swirled the water.
"What now!" Jade asked in fear, gripping her mother as she watched the answer approaching. Simon embraced Micky, pushing him behind his back then stepped in front of Therese and Jade.

An enormous asp turtle with long jagged tusks was stomping towards them, planting itself down onto the sea bed and digging his leather body into the sand leaving his island sized shell exposed. Objects began to grow from the lumps on the hard surface until a mass castle, looking as if it had been plucked straight out of a fairytale, sat on the back of the turtle, built entirely of seashells. An army of sea creatures swam out from the castle and approached carrying tridents that rang with melodious calls and whistles.

"Now that's what you call mermen," Ernset stated.

The family braced each other, not knowing what to do.

"This is it now go in the king knows you're here," Ernset flipped, calling Gillicus to join him, he left, swimming back towards the direction they had come.

Surrounding the family, the mermen ordered they swim forward, guiding them towards the direction of the throne galley, with clenched green teeth. The family stared at the creatures in curiosity. The mermen had silver-grey bodies, the scales became more defined in the lower half of their tails. Tufts of green seaweed flowed from their heads, some with seaweed protruding beneath their noses and chins. Their eyes glowed an electric blue accented with eyelashes of seaweed. They were not the merpeople they had seen in picture books. They were quite slimy and fearsome.

The escorts led the family through the gates of the galley. They watched as more creatures appeared, carrying on with duties, cleaning, preparing giant clamshells with sea salads and a quartet making melodious sounds with coral instruments. The creatures were mermaids, and like the merman, they had the same skin, but their hair was metre long waves of mangled seaweed and their eyes were fluorescent pink in colour. A merman spoke asking the family to stand before a podium, in preparation to bow when the king approached.

The family stood awaiting the king when they felt a gush of water flow through the room, pushing their bodies backwards. They repositioned to gain their balance and with gaped mouths, they viewed the mass causing the currents. It was a huge black and white Orca, with distinctive patches moving very slowly and greeting his kingdom, led by a female serpent with a human head, red eyes and long red hair to match.

Therese, Simon, and Jade were prompted to bow by a merman. Then they carefully raised their heads, watching the killer whale lie on the podium.

The Orca greeted the family in a kindly and deep voice.

"I am Orcinus, the King of all waters." He spoke of Medwin with the utmost respect and showed concern for his disappearance.

Simon began to inform the object of their journey only to be interrupted by the orca, "You have no need to explain," a gush of bubbles nearly toppled them again. "I know what you need. What you seek can be found with me."

Therese and Simon looked at each other, both thinking, *I've got a bad feeling about this.*

The whale continued. "I have been in existence for many centuries and have learned much."

Jade watched, thinking, *he's not wrong, boy, is he old.* His thick leathery skin, stocky body and sickle shaped fin, wrinkled in rows like melting candles and his eyes showed deep knowledge.

"You must tell me something I do not know, if you wish to obtain the puzzle piece," Orcinus said.

Is that it! The family was relieved.

They all began to think, and Simon proceeded with his knowledge, explaining the theory of relativity. However, the King had already been educated with the information. Therese began her speech of politics but was disappointed to find the orca knew more.

It was Jades turn. "I know, I know! One day I met a penguin." The whale looked at her with curiosity, as she continued, "his name was Jack. But when he is in the desert, what do you call him?"

Simon and her mother looked over, *what penguin*?

King Orcinus lay on the podium, pondering the question, he was unable to find the answer.

Jade stretched a smile. "If he is in the desert you'd call him Lost!"

The whale thought about the answer for a moment, then exhaled a jet of laughter. A gush of water burst from his blowhole, shooting out the awaited puzzle piece.

"That was very good, child. You may take the piece and finish your task." Wishing them a careful journey, the orca departed.

The human headed serpent carried the piece, handing it to Simon and glared at him with her red eyes then departed with a hiss, to follow her king. The merman surrounded the family once again but this time they cheered, echoing pulses of whistles with their tridents. They led the family out of the kingdom and chanted goodbye, now shooting fireworks out of their tridents.

Simon took the lead and they proceeded to swim towards the exit when suddenly, a chill took hold of theirs bodies. Their clothes were now saturated and pulled them down with weight. They could feel themselves gasping as their lungs filled with water. In a panic, they all swam frantically towards the gateway with Micky clinging to his uncles' shirt. Relief emerged, when the impact of Ernset and his family grasped hold of their arms, dragging them to safety. The dolphins swam with intense speed through the ocean, then crashing through the wall of water, they re entered the tunnel.

The tunnel had filled with water now, as did their lungs, rapidly feeling the strain, the family needed to gasp oxygen. Simon was first to reach the exit, stretching for the knob, struggling to open the door due to the force of gushing water, pushing against him.

Florian removed her beak from Therese's arm and shouted, "Jade, you must make your wish, ask for the door to open."

Jade responded immediately, and within seconds, they felt the current push them to safety. The dolphins waved as they forced the door shut, then headed home.

Inside now, the family welcomed the air filling their lungs. They were floating but could feel the water subsiding as it cascaded through the orchard frame. Simon began to panic once again, realising he had lost the puzzle piece and was relieved to find it also floating above the water surface a short distance from Jade. The gush had forced it through the doorway.

"Thank goodness," Therese sighed, she felt the shallow waters and propped herself up, the glass like surface was nearly cleared. "Well, I guess we don't need baths now."

They all laughed and continued to inhale deep breaths of air.

Jade reached for the puzzle piece and began playing tug of war with Micky who fought a good struggle with many giggles to win the piece.

Jade suddenly stopped. "Wicks," she screamed in horror.

Tears began streaming from her eyes when she saw the limp body of Pickwick, floating unconscious upon the inch of water.

"Nooo," Therese wailed, tears began to stream down her face now.

Simon rushed to Pickwick, he gently scooped the tiny water-logged body into his palm, and the room went silent.

Chapter 15

THE BOUTIQUE

The family climbed to the second level. They all were stricken with grief.

Still holding the tiny drenched body, Simon pressed his smallest finger on Pickwick's chest and began a gentle pumping action. But nothing occurred, and no water was released. Unwilling to give up, Simon's eyes cornered with tears and he tried again and again, but there was still no reaction. Jade and Therese began to bawl with despair, Micky joined in seeing his family upset.

Topaz entered, and a frown crossed her face when she saw the reason for the anguish.

Therese, still streaming with tears, cried out, "Honey girl, your wish! You still have another one."

Jade did not wait for any more words. She made the wish and watched in hope as Simon opened his palm further, for all to see. "Please," she howled.

Pickwick jumped at the scream, shaking his waterlogged fur, "What is happened, why is you's crying?" he squeaked. "Pickwick was sleeping, me was, Pickwick miss it, me did, what is happened?"

They all stood in shock.

"WHAT!" bellowed Therese but delighted he was alive. "We thought you drowned, Jade made a wish. Hang on! Your wish," she at Jade, "you still have one more, Wicks was only sleeping."

"Whoo hoo," squealed Jade, she was so happy for both reasons, "now what should I wish for, um?"

Topaz cackled loudly, distracting her from the thoughts. "I think it would be best to keep it for another gateway. After all, you may require a wish and I see no need at this time."

Jade agreed then reached over aiding Pickwick to scurry onto her palm.

"Pickwick sorry, me am," he squeaked and hugged her finger. "Pickwick wants me Jade, me always be's with you."

Jade lifted her palm to her face and rubbed his fur on her cheek, as they giggled with contentment.

"It is wonderful to see happy faces again," Topaz said. "Now, what do you say to a boutique visit? I strongly believe a change of dry clothes, is in order." Topaz smiled at the drenched family, dripping puddles on the floor, "Now, off you go, get changed, gateway five awaits."

Off they went leaving a trail of water as they detoured to the puzzle board. Jade laid the piece in place and watched as the fourth piece fused with the others. Micky fluttered onto the board jumping on the finished section, giggling as he dodged Jade, who managed to grasp hold of his hand, and lead him to her mother.

"Come on you lot, let's get changed. After you." Therese said, allowing Jade to take the lead because she knew the way to the boutique from her last trip. Jumping in through the frame, Jade began to run towards her favourite store full of camo print clothes, when a kindly old hag named Habatrot approached, wearing a pillowed night cap, she used as a pin cushion.

"Well, hello again, little missy," Habatrot said. "Come for a change of threads, have you dear? I can see why," she smiled with deformed lips at the drenched family.

Habatrot greeted Therese and Simon, she took hold of Micky and squeezed a tight cuddle. Micky squealed with delight and played with her wiry grey hair, immediately taking a like to the old chubby woman. She directed Therese and Simon to the choices containing their sizes and politely insisted on helping Micky with a change of clothes.

"Come along, you little sprite," she chuckled at his fiddling. "Now don't you worry that pretty young head of yours, Miss Therese, I'll have him ready in a jiffy."

Therese and Simon headed towards the stores filled with outfits to suit their sizes and gender. The boutique was fantastic! Inside were shops housing rows of racks containing clothing, shoes, accessories and even novelty costumes. All made by Habatrot. It was like a shopping mall with no sale prices, everything was free!

Therese entered a trendy casual wear store. The house and each world were quite warm, so she selected a t-shirt, three quarter pants, as well as a pair of mock leather sandals. *Can't be genuine leather, we must save the animals,* she thought, knowing this would be her brothers' statement and he would be pleased with the choice. Simon on the other hand was not so casual with his selection, or better said, not so fashion conscious. He was delighted to find a hippie store and more delighted with his choice, a colourful tie dyed shirt and overly patterned pajama like pants.

Therese laughed at her brothers' attire. "You're such a dag," she said, walking into the shop then handed him a pair of joggers. "I reckon these would look better than those ugly things," she laughed even harder at his choice of rubber striped thongs, they were definitely overload.

Jade entered and giggled at her uncle's selection. "Boy, you really have bad taste when it comes to clothes. Now me, my taste rocks. You should let me be your fashion advisor." She wore a camo outfit, of course.

Simon rolled his eyes and laughed. Jades choice was definitely not for him, it was not bright enough, however, her lace up boots were pretty cool he would definitely wear them.

With everyone dressed in dry clothing, the family headed out ready for the next search and thanked the seamstress as they departed. Therese hugged Habatrot, pleased with the outfit the old woman had selected for her baby boy. Micky looked so cute, dressed in a pair of denim hot pants and a red striped shirt with a matching baseball cap. Therese planted kisses on his chubby cheeks, as he rubbed them off and giggled.

"Are you sure you know where the next gateway is?" Simon asked Jade.

"Have I been wrong yet? It's my room, I know, definitely, a hundred percent, for sure, absol…"

"Okay, okay, I get the message," Simon halted the extra versions of yes. Calling out he informed Topaz that they were leaving for the next task.

She ran to meet them wishing them luck and added, "I do believe, you will enjoy this one!"

Chapter 16

THE CANDY EXPERIENCE

The door watched as they approached, smiling as though it were in a contented bliss.

Suddenly, with an unexpected lively outburst, it began speaking rapidly, wobbling its obese face and squinting as chubby cheeks pushed against its eyes, announcing to the family how happy it was, how delighted, how excited, how gleeful, and how great it was to be a door, using synonyms to describe the same word over again.

"That's great," replied Simon, raising his eyebrow and twirling his finger beside his temple miming, 'it's crazy' to Therese. Then he turned the knob, opening the pink door to a field of snow.

"Oh cool, like really cool this time," exclaimed Jade. "Maybe we should've put snow gear on." They began the trek.

The air was quite warm; the snow was spongy, allowing them to bounce on it like a trampoline. The family stopped and decided to test the surface. Therese and Jade held hands and began jumping in sync with each other. Micky bounced and dropped onto his bottom, then tested other parts of his body as Simon leapt high, aiming to achieve a triple somersault before touching the surface. They all laughed and played for a short time until Simon made the decision to move on.

Bouncing their way along, the family continued versions of trampoline acrobatics until they felt the surface below give way and they began to fall into a deep trench, landing on the spongy surface at the bottom. Simon attempted to bounce in long leaps but found the trench wall too high; he was only able to reach past the halfway point.

"What now?" Therese dropped herself to a sitting position with Jade resting beside her.

In a moment of disappointment, Jade slapped the surface, scooping up a handful of the snow. Looking at it, she edged it to her nose, sniffing the substance. Then more curious, she risked a taste.
"It's marshmallow," she squealed. "Yum! Have a taste. It's weally, weally, goog," finishing her sentence with a mouthful.

Therese and Simon joined the taste test, reacting in surprise with the discovery.

"Wow," Therese said, "this is far out and boy it's a lot of marshmallow."

Jade finished her mouthful, "aha, it's heaps, how cool is this? I bet we could eat our way out," she helped herself to another scoop.

Simon disagreed. "How? We'll only make the hole bigger, it doesn't help us get up there," he looked up and pointed, viewing the hole. "Shoot! What was that!" he bellowed with fright, catching a glimpse of white fur.

Stepping in front of the family, Simon veered them into a huddle, as a long red, rubbery rope fell to his feet. Not wanting to touch it, Simon called out, "who are you, are you here to help?"

A strong voice echoed down from the cavity. "It will be okay. Please take hold of the licorice and I will guide you up. I mean you no harm."

Simon grasped hold and the rope began to lift him up the ditch wall. "Just wait until I see what's happening. Don't do anything until I say it's okay," he called to Therese.

Now at the top, Simon's heart pounded when he saw a hand of stark white skin take hold of his own hand and pull him to the surface.

"I do apologize, kind sir, I hope nobody was hurt. I set these traps to contain the snotlings, not humans. Snotlings are pests in our world. Their appetites are quite large for their tiny bodies, devouring the lands like termites in your world."

Simon stood still with astonishment, ogling the pure white creature towering before him, covered in a coat of soft mohair, with feet the size of a coffee table, yet it had the handsome face of a human.

"Ar-, are you a yeti?" Simon asked in fascination.

The creature expelled a deep chuckle. "Sometimes, I suppose, depending on your mythology books; however, I prefer Sasquatch. It is an honour to meet you. My name is Brig. Now! Shall I retrieve the others?"

Simon nodded and then bellowed, advising Therese it was safe to come up. Micky fluttered ahead, and Therese held Jade during their lift to the surface, both were taken aback, just as Simon had been, when they initially saw Brig.

Jade's shock lasted briefly, and she cheered with excitement, discovering that yetis really did exist, excelling her desire in search of archeology and now legends. She stared in thought at the large beast

"Is that really licorice?" and receiving a positive response, she chewed off an end. "Yummm, it is, and berry flavoured too. It's my favourite! I like this place so far."

Brig chuckled once again, "so far, hmm, then I gather you will enjoy the other parts of this world. After all, it is made entirely of candy."

Jade screeched with delight at the thought, Micky joined in, simply for fun, and Wicks slapped his forehead.
"Pickwick will have much cleaning to do, me's will," he shook his head.

Simon informed the Sasquatch of their task and learned that the head gnome would be the one to ask. Brig offered to guide the family through the field of marshmallow to avoid other traps he had laid and they all agreed, particularly Jade, who took hold of his large white thumb, still popping with excitement, whilst Micky fluttered up to a hairy shoulder and planted himself on the gentle creature.

Brig led the trek. Therese and Simon jogged to keep up. His long strides made them pant and wish they had built up their fitness levels as they passed fields of fairy floss trees, lollypops, and feathered trees with growths of gummy lollies. With swift agility, Brig gently clamped Micky with two fingers, feeling the squirm, as Micky prepared to dart off into the forests.

"Wait a moment, little one. There will be plenty of samples at the castle," he said and chuckled at Jades heavenly expression.

Therese smiled with relief, thinking, *boy, he'd be a great babysitter. I need to get myself a yeti.*

They passed more candy forests and the family stared with amazement as cheery, white haired gnomes, about two feet tall, wearing red, purple, and pink togas, attended to their tasks. The little men looked much like the statues, nestled in the garden of their world, except only a few had trimmed beards, and some were bald. The gnomes, plucked sweets from the trees and candy patches, sang songs to the smaller growths, and danced merrily about the fields beneath arrays of sparkles, shooting above like fireworks.

"Canderlas," Brig informed the family. "Tiny sprites, very humanlike in form. Their bodies illuminate and appear as twinkling lights, similar to the fire flies in your world, they live by heat and are drawn to this world because of the river," he pointed at the bubbling waterway that branched into canals, steaming with boiling hot syrup.

More gnomes tottered beside the canals collecting syrup, and passed the jugs along a production line, that emptied the contents into dams of artificial colouring. There were other groups in lollypop forests, stepping on candy cane ladders, measuring growth size, adding sprinkles of sugar to the roots, and others pruned vines of tangled liquorice.

Mobile floats decorated with candied flowers, drove across vacant fields, carrying gnomes who tossed heart shaped seeds followed by others holding watering cans full of syrup, watering the sows.

They continued scanning the sights as they walked over a candied slat bridge. Looking down, Therese and Jade felt butterflies in the pits of their stomach, as the river of clear syrup, edged with crystallized rocks, boiled furiously beneath them. Reaching the end of the bridge, they sighed with relief, including Simon and Brig. The ground was now surfaced with pebbles of hard boiled lollies. Jade and Micky were drooling, spying the large, clear barrels made of the hardened syrup, lined in rows encasing mountains of candy, some with lollypops poking out like umbrella stands. This place was a sugar-coated heaven.

Brig jerked his head sideways and quickly placed Micky down. "I have them now." Stomping in haste he called out, "go to the castle and seek an audience with Tocs. He is the head gnome. Goodbye and good luck." Brig's voice disappeared in the distance.

The Sasquatch had darted off to catch the tiny, orange skinned creatures with oval heads and pink button noses. They had no ears and bodies of a rabbit they also hopped the same.

"Bye, thank you," bellowed Simon, "and before you ask, they were Snotlings, they're the termites of this world." That closed the open jaws of Therese and Jade. "Come on. Let's go, there's the castle." Simon led the way.

"This is the coolest," Jade yelled when they neared the tall structure. "Why can't we live in a candy castle or even a gingerbread castle? At least you wouldn't have to cook, mum."

Therese laughed and helped the children scoop a hand full of gummy lollies, from a barrel. "Because you two would have sugar overload and get really hypo. It's enough keeping up with Micky as it is."

The castle had no front door, only an opening covered in a curtain of boiled lolly strips. Pushing across the beaded strips to enter, Jade and Micky giggled when the lollies knocked together sounding like a chime. A gnome wearing a layered toga and ornate spectacles, decorated with sugar diamantes, totted over to greet them.

"Well hello sugars, welcome to candy castle. I am Klink," he said in a festive voice, also inviting them to feast on assortments of sweets within the castle.

Simon asked for the head gnome. Klink curtsied and led them up a floating spiral staircase, with spongy steps and licorice handrails.

Entering the room above, they saw an obese gnome wearing a bright pink toga with garlands of licorice around his neck and a crown of hard-boiled lollies sat askew on top of his bald head. It was Tocs, the head gnome, completing his work on tissue-thin fairy floss paper with a pen that wrote in a candy ink.

"Welcome, welcome, sweeties," he greeted them with jovial enthusiasm and waddled towards them, shaking the thumb of Simon, then Therese, both bowed, to help him to reach their hands. "I hope you honeypops are enjoying the fruits of our labour. After all, a sweet tooth is our favourite tooth." Tocs giggled like a jackhammer.

He looked over at Jade and Micky stacked with piles of samples they had collected along the way and clapped his chubby hands together, pleased to see some fans. Pickwick was frantically wiping Micky's chin of the sticky residue and waiting for a hand to empty.

Simon began the explanation for their visit and asked for any aid in the search, only to be told that the puzzle piece was in the second field of lollypops they had passed. The family thanked the gnome for his cheerful hospitality and headed out of the castle, back tracking their way to the forest.

'Aww, do we have to go? Can't we just live here?" Jade asked in a disappointed voice, knowing the answer but insisted it was worth a try.

Therese placed her arm around Jade's shoulder and rubbed her fist playfully into her head. "I don't think we need to. I mean look at the lifetime supply of candy you two monkeys have."

They laughed as they approached the forest, spread with rows full of assorted lollypops and all began searching about for the puzzle piece.

"There it is," Jade pointed to a candy perched on a stick of musk.

It was the puzzle piece, hidden amongst the other lollypops.

"Yee ha," cheered Simon. "Now you lot start heading back to the exit. I'll wait until you're near it before I pluck it off."

Therese began to disagree, but Simon stopped the argument, pleading that they begin the trek back. Finally agreeing, Therese grasped Micky and took hold of Jade's hand and they began the walk, heading back to the gateway.

"Let's follow our footprints in the marshmallow, mum," Jade said, "so we don't fall into another snotling trap." It was a good idea.

Meanwhile Simon waited and counted, "one, one hundred, two, one hundred…" He continued to eighty before plucking the puzzle piece. It was definitely enough time for his sister and the kids to reach the exit.

Therese stood at the door then turned the knob. She guided the children through and waited by the open door watching for her brother to return. Jade stood nearby, and both began to worry.

Simon plucked the tree, immediately feeling the rumble beneath his feet. He tucked the piece under his arm and broke into a sprint towards the gateway.
The marshmallow surface began to crack and split into segments like icebergs, floating on a sea of hot liquid

syrup. Simon used each segment as a stepping-stone, skipping from one to another when a surge of panic threatened his composure. His stepping stones were melting as the hot syrup rose.

"Run, Uncle Simon!" yelled Jade when she spotted her uncle, almost chewing her nails as she watched.

The stepping-stones continued to shrink as Simon neared the exit, making his balance quite weak, but he persisted with intense focus.

"Four more only, quick," Therese was pulling her hair from the tension. "Two more…"

Simon landed on the second last one, barely the size of his shoe, gasping in pain as the searing heat of the syrup burnt through to his foot. Looking ahead, he watched as the last step disappeared. There was no way he could make the jump and the segment beneath him was dissolving rapidly. Then Jade remembered her wish.

"Please Amiya, I need you. I ask for a path, so my uncle can get to the exit."

Simon was smiling as he limped along the new path, then through the doorway. Closing the door, he turned to Jade and opened his arms to embrace his hero.

"Thanks squirt, you're the best," he smiled through clenched teeth. "I just need to ask you one more favour."

Placing his weight on one leg, he pointed to his burnt foot and melted shoe.
"A dose of your healing power would be really great."

Jade gasped and reacted immediately, she touched a left stone, somehow knowing it was the one for the cure. Within moments, her uncle stood on both feet, feeling no pain, and no scar was visible, but he did need a new shoe.

"Thanks," Therese said and hugged her brother, still shaken, "I'm glad the kids didn't go through that one. Here, I'll put the piece in place, you go to the boutique and get some shoes."

Therese took the puzzle piece from Simon and walked off with Micky fluttering ahead. He wanted to jump on the game board again. She stopped when she heard Topaz.

"WHAT ARE YOU DOING HERE?" the possum hollered from another room.

Chapter 17

THE VAULTED FRAME

The family sprinted to see the problem and gasped when they entered the living room

Therese stopped, a feeling of guilt flushed through her. It was her fault. She had kept the door open to watch Simon and was distracted by the drama. She did not see the snotling sneak past.

There was a trail of sugar leading to the position where the creature stood, rummaging through the container as it devoured the contents. Pickwick scurried with a cloth wiping the trail, aiming for the culprit. The snotling froze, staring back at the ogling crowd and then began scampering about with hyperactive speed as it crashed into furniture and stumbled over smaller objects.

"Quickly, everyone. We must capture it, or it will damage many things in sight," Topaz bellowed.
The family began the pursuit, diving and aiming to corner it.

Finally, after a frantic chase, the snotling was caught. It was the wrought iron pot that succeeded; it had tossed itself directly at the creature and secured it within. Topaz breathed a sigh of relief asking Simon to gather the creature and follow her. Therese and the children also followed, curious about the possum's destination.

Climbing through a frame they had not yet seen, Topaz led the family down a corridor of towering iron vaults leading to a wide, open space. Reaching the end, they found all walls stacked with glass cages and floating steps that moved like a flexible ladder, stretching to the higher cubed prisons.

"Place the snotling in this one," Topaz pointed a claw at the large glass box.

Simon inserted the creature into the cell as tears edged Jades eyes.

"Will it be okay? she asked. "The box hasn't got any air holes."

Topaz smiled at her concern, "it will be completely fine. These cages are made of crystal and are quite porous. It has plenty of space and most importantly, this snotling cannot destroy the house while it is contained. It can be your pet, until we can return it to world of candy. The only downfall now is you will have to share your sweets; that is all it eats, and plenty of it, I might add."

Jade smiled in return, agreeing to feed her new pet and was quite happy to share the treats from the candy corner.

Walking back to exit the frame, Therese detoured to the side and rubbed her palm against a vault.

"What's inside these things, are they safes," she asked Topaz.

"Oh. They are enchanted vaults, to be exact. Each one contains currency from different worlds. There is one with paper and metal cash from your world. Medwin kept a store for his finances. It is what you would call a bank."

Lifting their jaws off the floor from shock, Simon asked if they had access to the money.

"Absolutely," replied Topaz. "Although, it is Therese only who can enter these vaults."

"WHAT!" screeched Therese. "But, how?"

"Well," Topaz looked up at the ceiling that seemed to stretch forever, once again jogging her memory. "Oh yes. You must match the surface and this will enable you to see the combination in your conscious mind. So, you see! Therese, you can only determine the combination when are camouflaged, your power is truly an asset."

Therese grinned widely, "Finally! Yee ha! annd... I got the best job, the finance controller," she cheered. "I was beginning to think my power was useless."

Jade held her mother's hand as they headed for gateway six, rubbing her belly she complained, "mum, I feel a bit sick. I think I'm gonna throw up."

Therese looked at her pale daughter. "I knew you'd get sick. You and Micky went overboard on lollies. Come here, honey girl." She comforted Jade with a hug, adding, "I think we should rest for an hour or so, before we enter the next gateway."

Simon agreed he too felt a little drained from the last gateway and Therese led her children to the master bedroom to prepare for a nap.

Tucking the kids in, Therese remembered the cushion and removed it from her pocket. She asked for a stomach ache potion. Then pulling her hand out, she held a silver mug, containing a brown gluey substance and gave it to Jade.

"Yuk!" Jade complained. "Please mum, I don't want to drink it. It looks gross."

But her mother insisted, advising that it would make her feel better and watched as Jade skulled the contents.

"Not bad! Jade said, wiping the corners of her mouth. "It tastes like macaroni cheese. I like this medicine."

The potion did not really taste like the pasta dish. It always released a favourite flavour, making the substance quite delicious for the person who was holding the mug.

Snores echoed through the house within minutes; the family had expended a lot of energy during their treks, not realising how exhausted they actually were.

Their dreams reappeared. This time Therese had visions of herself, blending to match fabrics and stones. In the dream, she was excited, because she acquired the knowledge to become one with the objects she encountered. Waking, she yawned.

"That's it," she said aloud. "I just need to recognise the elements that make up an object. Cool! Now I'm definitely camo woman."

The children awoke to their mother's voice. Catching the last sentence, Jade giggled. "Cool bananas, so you had a good dream eh?" she said, "nice to meet you, camo mum!" and they both laughed at the nickname.

Walking out of the bedroom, Therese turned her focus to the fabric of the cushion and managed to transform herself into the interlocked weaves almost mimicking the object. *Practice makes perfect* she thought and studied her skin. Jade looked at her mother, a little shocked at her appearance but not too concerned.

"Mmm what's that smell?" asked Jade, as they headed for the kitchen. It made her hungry.

"Ah, hello sleeping beauties, all well and fresh, I see," Topaz was leaning over the fry pans containing the aromatic smell. "I thought you may be slightly hungry after the nap, so I prepared a batch of 'Toad in a hole'." Jade poked her tongue out in disgust. "Relax, my dear. It is simply fried bread, with a hole cut in the centre, containing an egg. Surely you do not think I would cook real frogs," the possum smirked.

Both Therese and Jade sighed with relief as a dish anxiously scrambled in front, waiting for them to eat.

"Well, come on you two, the eggs are quite fresh. I attended the farmyard portrait during your forty winks and collected them myself." Topaz began nibbling her serve.

Simon entered, stretching he spied the food and scratched his head. Jade was eating without complaint it must be good.

"Should I ask?" Simon looked at his sister, contemplating the question of what he was about to eat. Therese shook her head. "Great. I'm starving."

"It's pretty good," Therese nudged her daughter, "and there's definitely no frogs in it." Jade laughed along with her mother.

Simon began his feast confused with the joke.

All but Simon had finished their meal. "Dish cloths," Topaz called out, ordering the sponges to clean the empty plates as Pickwick cleaned Micky and other cloths wiped the bench. Simon swallowed his last bite and stretched, satisfied from the meal.

"I guess it's time for door six." He still sat on the stool his thoughts began to wonder. "There's something that's been bugging me though," he looked at Topaz, his expression showed a look of concern. "When the gateways collapse, melt or whatever. What happens to the inhabitants?"

"Oh, nothing," replied the possum casually.

"What do you mean by nothing?" Therese was annoyed by the blasé response.

"Do not be concerned," Topaz said. "Nothing occurs to the worlds or to the inhabitants as a matter of fact. When the puzzle piece is removed, a protective bubble is created, and a parallel existence appears in a fraction of a second, without you knowing it. Quite simply put, the world you are in becomes an illusion and changes to another even though they are identical."

"Thank goodness!" exclaimed Therese. "Gosh, that illusion stuff is head bending but it's pretty amazing!"
"Well, off you go then, your next adventure awaits," urged Topaz. "Good luck but remember this. Not all creatures are kind. Be sure to stay sharp."

Jade led the family to the next gateway. "Oh, wow," she said, standing before the red entry, "it's really sparkly."

Chapter 18

QUEEN FARACY'S PALACE

The door glistened like a Christmas star, and snoozed with a smile. It continued to sleep as Simon opened the gateway, finding a row of giant lily pads aligned on a wide, glittering lake.

Everyone stepped upon the first leaf. Therese closed the door then turned to see the reason for the awes, voiced by Simon and Jade. The surrounding landscape was captivating, so beautiful and serene. The sound of celestial music strummed from above the blueberry skies. Tall multi coloured toadstools shadowed the embankment to one side of the lake. The remaining water's edge housed groves of oak trees, draping willows, and ferns, all, growing on beds of bluebells, forget-me-nots, and tulip blooms.

"Gosh," exclaimed Therese, "I think we've found Eden, it's..." she paused to yawn, "like a paradise. Jeepers, I'm still tired. I could fall asleep on this spot."

She looked over to her family and saw they too were yawning as their eyelids began to droop.

"Stop it," she yelled. "Wake up, shake your head, slap your face, whatever. Remember what Topaz said? Stay sharp! We can't go to sleep, something's trying to force it." Therese shook her head in order to stay awake and grabbed the folded cushion. "Anti-sleep potion, please. And fast!"

This time it was not the mug containing sludge, but a small box filled with red dust. Therese was not sure how to apply it but time was not in her favour, so she tossed the contents over herself and each family member. In an instant, everyone felt alert and prepared for what was ahead then Jade screeched.

"Look," she pointed, "wh-, what are they?"

Creatures in the form of mermaids leapt from the lake and nosedived like dolphins, as they chanted a ghostly verse,

"come with us. We shall take thee away, into a land where the Merrow all play."

They were not mermaids at all. They were in fact leeching Merrow, a vanity driven race that only see beauty in their reflection, even though they have the face of a hog, with grey teeth, moss green hair, and obese human bodies that contour to a slim fish tail. They disliked any race that challenged their belief that they were beautiful. The chants began to affect the family as their thoughts drifted off in a trance. Suddenly, the lake began to harden, freezing the Merrow within and some in midair.

"Do not be alarmed," they could hear a soft voice say within their minds, "we have arrived to help."

Ice maidens with skin of pale blue and ankle length hair to match, wearing flowing white gowns, skated with grace on the iced lake with bare feet, heading towards the family, using telepathy to speak. They were sickly thin and inches taller than Simon, but their faces were stunning with carved petite features.

"Come, take our hands, we shall lead you from the lake," echoed the ice maidens.

Micky fluttered to a younger looking maiden, allowing her to embrace him and the rest of the family took the hands of their guides.

"Welcome to the forest of myths, where many wondrous creatures dwell. Our queen, Faracy, controls the harmony. Do not be afraid, we shall aid in your trek to Archelon Palace."

The family glided along the lake with ease, poised by the maidens, holding hands that were surprisingly quite warm for their icy appearance. It was a joyous skate, up until creatures began appearing from the thick growths and floral petals. It was quite intimidating, yet exciting to be surrounded by masses of unusual creatures.

"Oh cool," shouted Jade as she watched butterfly fairies crawl out of the moss, from the rock walls barricading the lake. They were shy and lovely, slender humanlike sprites with coloured wings of a butterfly. She turned her attention to other creatures that equally surprised her.

There was Fairy like Devas, with fluid bodies, flying out of tulip petals, transforming into small spheres of light. Winged, Ghilly wood nymphs with a filmy appearance peeled themselves off tree trunks, wearing armour of bark. Short, brown face Otteer goblins, with, long hair, long teeth, and curled nails, came drenched out of water falls that cascaded from the open sky, wearing clothes made of foxglove petals and shelled hats. Hideous half man, half horse creatures, with fins for feet, leapt out of the lake on the embankment, emitting the smell, of rotten fish. The family braced themselves, hearing the maiden's voice, echo.

"Newo's. They will not harm you."

But the stench ridden creatures wore sullen and grouchy expressions, which added fear for the family.

Nearing the edge of the lake, Therese, Simon, and Jade watched as a man stood waiting with antlers of a stag, holding a pipe. He was a handsome creature with an aristocratic stance, wearing a blinding white cloth. His youthful, soft-skinned face was accented by long golden hair. The family was in awe of him.

"Greetings," he said, with a smile. "I hope you are enjoying the forest. My name is Alfiem, I will guide you from here. The ice maidens cannot walk on land, so they must leave you now."

He bowed to the maidens as they transformed into water, vanishing within seconds. Jade and Micky were disappointed. They had fun skating and soon realised they had to jump, because the ice melted below their feet.

"Come this way," Alfiem prompted the family to stand beside him. "We need that clearing, beyond the oaks, that is where you begin your next trek." He pointed to a mass of land, cleared of tall vegetation with only a carpet of wild flowers spread about.

They arrived at the clearing in an instant. Alfiem had played somewhat of a marching tune on his pipe and this transported everyone to the location.
"Wow." Therese was surprised but a little shocked. She rubbed her stomach feeling a slightly nauseated. Though their trip was only seconds, the world around them had become animated and time seemed to stand still. "Thank goodness it's back to normal," she said. "Well normal for this world anyway."

Simon was not startled at all. "I've got to get me one of those pipes," he loved any musical instrument and a magical one was a bonus!

Alfiem smiled then once again placed his pipe to his lips and played a squawking tune that almost deafened the family. Within moments, the family could see what the tune attracted.

A flight of winged maidens, their torso covered in tan feathers, with old crone heads and sharp talons approached, casting a shadow over the herd of Catobass grazing by a near spring. The four-legged Catobass had a bull like appearance, with a furred mane falling across their heads and bodies covered in crocodile scales. The maidens ceased their flight as they landed in front of Alfiem, squawking in bird like voices to greet him and the family.

"The harpies will take you to Archelon palace. It is suspended high above, held up by a vine of entangled thorns. It is not possible to climb. The assassin spikes will poison you in an instant."

Alfiem bowed and the harpies each clamped a family member within their talons, taking off in flight once again.

"Whooo Hooo!" the family cheered as they soared through the sky.

They were having the time of their life, stretching their arms as if flying whilst listening to the harpies squawk information on the surroundings below. "Those wells down there, house water pixies. Those trees grow mallow fruit and that cluster grows pixie pears. That glass harp over yonder is played to bring about the four seasons. Those huts over there belong to all sorts of fairies depending on what they like. Some like to build them of twigs, dried grass and leaves; others prefer flat river stones, and those huts down there are made from acorns. That mound of crystal, near those cabbage stalks, is the home of the Mine Trolls. A helpful lot they are."

It was fantastic; they had never known there were so many species of creatures and fairies, particularly the ones with feathered hair and wings. Therese pointed to a group of creatures. "What the heck are those?" she asked.

They were ugly and withered looking, somewhere between a goblin and a fairy with scraggly hair and mismatched limbs.

"Crimbils," squawked the harpies. "Nasty little beasts. They are shape shifters and smell awful. You can always tell if they have transformed because the stench still fills the air. Avoid them at all costs."

Passing through a large cloud of smoke, they saw the palace come into view. It was a spectacular mix of organically shaped towers, made entirely of opaque crystal with sparkling gems embedded on the façade. The harpies released the family smoothly on the ground. The surface was a flow of water but felt solid to walk on.

"Go on then," they squawked. "We shall wait for your return. The Coltpixies will help you now."

Well! That's a relief, Therese thought; at least they had a way of getting off the cloud.

Walking forward they watched, as two tall crystal doors vanished, allowing them entry. Once inside they gasped to see the interior and its contents also made entirely of gems and crystal, with numerous stairwells leading to podiums. One central podium housed a silver throne encased with diamonds, sitting on a carpet of flower petals.

"Hello, new friends," came high pitched voices. "Drink this honey milk. The queen awaits, hurry now," ordered little red fairies with round black eyes and curly black hair.

The fairies handed each member a goblet, filled with the creamy liquid and waited impatiently as the family drank.

"Yum," Jade wiped her top lip with her sleeve. She was definitely going to have milk more often now, with honey of course.

Suddenly, the family felt weightless, their feet floated slightly above the surface. Groups of Coltpixies grasped hold of each member, lifting them by their clothes and fluttered up to the podium where the throne sat.

"Ouch stop it!" yelled Simon, after he felt numerous pinches from the fairies that carried him.

"Ouch!" yelled Jade, so did her mother. They too were pinched.

Micky laughed as though it was a tickle, whilst Pickwick covered himself with Jade's fingers to hide from the little buggers.

The Coltpixies landed the family onto the throne podium, all adding another pinch before they returned to their duties.

"Mischievous little creatures are they not?"

The enchanting, almost bewitching voice bounced off the crystal walls and echoed. A graceful woman appeared, a tower over Simon's height, with wings of specter flowing in a gentle ghostly mist.

"They do so like to play," she looked at the family, but not Simon. "Greetings, I am Faracy, Queen of Archelon."

She was strikingly beautiful, with pale skin that highlighted clear violet eyes, surrounded by long silver lashes. She wore a diamond gown that glimmered as she glided and a silver diadem, embedded with a ruby on her head of lavender flowing hair. Simon began to speak, and then stopped. The queen ignored him. It was as though he was invisible.

"Undry," Faracy called, watching as a silver cauldron appeared between them. "I have been expecting you. Medwin sought that I care for the item you need." She continued with another call saying, "scroll, return to the hands of the woman before me."

A papyrus scroll flew out of the cauldron and floated to Therese, resting itself upon her palm.
Therese looked at the rough paper, confused she asked, "but, we came for a puzzle piece, not this scroll. I can't even read it. What do these symbols mean?"

Faracy smiled at her, "there is no puzzle piece in this world. Medwin has only left the scroll. You must decipher it in order to succeed another task ahead. Now, you must go, you have much to do. You will be returned safely to the gateway."

The Queen disappeared in a ghostly mist and goblets containing the honey milk appeared in the hand of each family member. "Drink," the bewitching voice echoed. And they did.

The Coltpixies returned the family to the awaiting Harpies, who in turn guided them back to the gateway and showed sympathy for the painful number of pinches each member had received from the little imps. The Harpies landed the family beside the doorway and much like a kiss they gently pecked all five including Pickwick then flew off, squawking their goodbyes.

Therese stood on the giant lily pad, the scroll safe in her hand. She looked at her family, all but Micky were sombre. No puzzle piece, they were disappointed.

"Come on you guys, let's go work this clue out," she said in a happy voice trying to cheer Simon and Jade. "You know, I reckon it was pretty fun. That flying was excellent and what about all those creatures? It really was worth coming here."

They looked at her, smiles stretching across their faces. She was right, it was fun, and they would definitely return to this world.

Simon, however, still felt a surge of disappointment. It seemed as though the queen disliked him, and he could not understand why. Entering, he closed the door and called for Topaz.

Chapter 19

BRAIN BENDERS BEGIN

"Well, nice to see you all. Did you have fun? I can see you have obtained the scroll. Good show. How is Faracy?" Topaz stood before them now with a smile.

Simon answered with a frown. "It was pretty great, but I'm sure Faracy and some of the other creatures as a matter of fact, ignored me, I just don't know why."

Topaz explained that fairies disliked iron. Therefore, the cuff Simon wore would have been a terrible sight for these creatures.

"Do not concern yourself, though. They do know it was not your choice, they simply cannot look at it. Oh, and by the way, there are still three more doors left to complete. There are eight puzzle pieces in total, in case you were wondering." Topaz jerked for a moment and pointed to Simon. "Oh dear, not another one," she directed Simon to the tiny blue, scaled frog, clamped on his shirt.

"Great! This is becoming a real habit." Simon reached over his shoulder and grasped the creature.

Topaz began the trek, leading the family to the vaults, intending to encase the leace in a crystal cage. "Well, I guess you have yet another pet," the possum said to Jade.

"Whoo hoo," Jade was elated. "But, do we have to put him in that box? Can't I keep him with me?" she pleaded.

Topaz shook her head. "Absolutely not! Simon was quite lucky; if this little fellow had bitten him, he would have a very painful blister now. It would not be permanent though or cause any other damage, just a few hours of intense pain."

Simon nearly dropped the leace on hearing this and raced to the rear corridor when they entered the frame, placing the creature into the closest container.

"It's really cute," Jade cooed and watched through the crystal glass. It seemed happy enough. The frog jumped about and somersaulted.

Topaz chuckled. "Well at least you have one now. I recall not that long ago when you asked your mother if you could keep that garden toad."

What! exclaimed Therese. "But, that was a giant cane toad."

"Ah, so you thought," Topaz said. "Medwin collected leace from the mythical forest and bewitched them to appear as toads, he also added a growth spell. He placed them about the yard, hoping to deter others from entering the property, in particular, the home buyers. However, they began to multiply rapidly; hence, the infestation in the other areas. This, we did not foresee and most definitely did not plan."

They all shrugged. It was not so surprising they had already experienced many shocks. Therese led the way out of the frame, she glimpsed at the leace and shuddered.

"Yuk!" she still thought they were ugly. "So, what do you reckon, are you guys up to decoding?" Therese fluttered her eyelashes as if to say please.

Simon and Jade agreed, and they headed for the lounge room whilst Micky and Pickwick darted off to play a game of chase. "Stay close," his mum called out.

Therese unrolled the scroll and they put their heads together ready to work on the inscription.

✦9πΛ≅ ✔ υρεψ 7ε◁△eαΛ ✔ ηε δεΤΤεΡσ ✔ κ ♋≅εν ✔ ηε ΨαΤε♒αφ

"What the heck does it say?" Jade asked, confused at the symbols and letters before her. "It looks like it's written in Chinese or something."

Jade was half right, something it was, but what!

"Let's work out the letters we sort of know, first," suggested Simon.

Therese called for a piece of paper and a desk galloped in, opening its drawer containing a pad and fountain pens.

"Thanks," she said, and she gripped the pieces, "I could get used to this. Now it's something, something, then a U, I think."

She began writing out the letters, with Simon and Jade's suggestions, leaving dashes for some they were unsure of.

"I think the ticks represent a t," suggested Jade and they read the sentence with the t in place. "So, if the ticks start with t, maybe that star looking thing stands for s, and those two rings are r or something."

Simon agreed, suggesting the box with an arrow looked like an upside-down v and the last word had a back to front g. Therese began to read out the sentence with their new discoveries.

"Sculqtures reveal the –etters to –qen the gate-aj," she finished.

"That's not a q, that's a p and I reckon the squiggles are a w," stated Simon and he became excited. "Sculptures reveal the something to something the gatewaj. Whoo hoo! We're close."

Thinking for a moment, Jade spotted an abstract sculpture sitting within a niche. "I'll bet you it's those. Each one has a letter." She pointed, then correcting her uncle, she smiled and said, "Sculptures reveal the letters to open the gateway."

They all jumped up running about the house collecting the clues carved on the artworks.

"Great," Simon complained, "another code."

Each piece had a letter engraved and placed together it spelt 't.h.e.i.s.' it made no sense. Therese, Simon and Jade sat on the floor, disappointed with their find. All three lost in their thoughts. No one reacted when Topaz approached.

"Why the glum looks?" she asked. "You do not need to solve this yet. I suggest you all give your brains a rest and prepare for gateway seven."

Relieved of the brain teaser, Therese stood up and headed for Micky. He was busy playing tag with Pickwick and was the chaser of course. Therese began to jump about until she caught Micky in flight. He struggled and giggled thinking his mother was now playing the game. Jade had followed, her mind still pondering the clues from the sculptures and found Pickwick catching his breath after the last chase. She stretched out her arm, allowing Picks to scurry onto her palm and they all began to walk toward the next gateway.

Chapter 20

KNOWLEDGE IN RIDDLES

"Good wishes to you," said the green door as they approached. "May your journey bring fortune of knowledge."

It was a curious door, portraying a face of a wise old man wearing spectacles beneath hairy grey eyebrows. Simon greeted him, then turned the handle anti clockwise once consent was received. The family entered, closing the door behind them.

"Far out!" exclaimed Simon, "That's a lot of trees."

They stood at the foot of a towering bookshelf, with endless height. Each shelf contained books from all categories of literature.

"They're books now, you big greenie," Therese said, rubbing her brother's shoulders. "At least these trees were used for something useful, look at Jade she's happy."

Jade was elated and scanned many of the classics, feeling like she was in library heaven.

"Ouch," Simon felt three books stub his foot.

The hardcover novels fell from the lowest shelf, he should have picked the steel-capped boots Habatrot offered instead of the open toe sandals. Each book began to rumble then opened, revealing the first page. The author's name floated out and began transforming into distorted figures of three people. The first to appear in whole was a woman with a large nose and brown hair tied into a loose bun.

"Good day, to you all," she said. "You must seek the hidden piece within these books to complete your journey. I shall aid you with a clue, and my colleagues shall grant you two more."

An old male transformed, wearing a pin stripped suit with unkempt silver hair and overgrown facial hair, followed by another male, years younger, with light brown cropped hair, also wearing a suit that was not quite tailored. He had a jolly nature and a face to match.

The woman began to speak her clue, "it marks your way and aids increases," followed by the elderly man saying, "it freely moves to your position." The younger man smiled then said, "a page can be found when I am the guide," he winked and disappeared. All three returned, morphing back to the book from where they came.

"What!" bellowed Simon, "is that it? Not another brain teaser. I guess the last trip was a warm up. I want them to say it again, I forgot the first bits."

Jade tugged on her uncles' shirt. "It's okay. I remember all of it. You're just lucky I'm here, eh?" she smiled, pretending to hold her head together as if it grew.

Jade began to repeat the words as they thought, searching for a meaning, unable to find an answer with the combinations of mixed ideas.

"Let's just climb the shelves," suggested Therese. "Maybe we have to check all the books but read the spines first. You never know what could happen."

Both agreed, and Jade placed Pickwick on her shoulder, allowing both hands free to climb the shelves. Now ready, they began ascending the tower with Micky hovering near his mother.

They scanned through the hundreds of spines, passing fiction novels, picture books, encyclopedias, and non-fiction books and were no closer to solving the clues or even reaching the top of the tower. It seemed to grow the farther they climbed. Simon was curious, so without hesitation, he pulled out a guide to fishing and it was only when he opened it his curiosity turned to regret. A gush of water forced him back and fish popped out slapping him in the face.

"Thank goodness," Therese sighed, as she watched her brother catch the edge of a shelf, securing his drop but drenched from the wash.

The water and fish vanished before hitting the surface at the foot of the shelf, whilst the book slammed itself shut and hurried back to its original place. Micky watched, giggling with excitement then grabbed a farmyard picture book, he hoped something would fall out of it too. Therese hurried across to stop him but was too late. Cows, chickens, and sheep shot out and began to fall; sounding their common noises, then disappeared as the fish had.

"Nooo..." her voice echoed when Micky took hold of more books releasing teddy bears, the alphabet, fairies, cartoon characters, cars, and bugs.

Simon and Jade braced onto the shelves below, dodging the objects and characters that fell past them. Therese managed to sneak up beside her cheeky son and with a rapid swoop, she caught him, pulling him from the shelf and holding him at a distance, just in time. He had focused his attention towards a series of novels containing monsters.

"You two keep checking," Therese said. "I need to hold Micky. I'll edge down and wait down the bottom."

She descended the shelf slowly and with much discomfort, she struggled with Micky, who wiggled and tugged, trying to break free.

Simon and Jade continued the search, perusing the spines in hope of finding the answer to the clue. Jade climbed to the next shelf, filled with classics. Reading from right to left, she stopped a quarter of the way, in thought, she looked at a Mark Twain novel. Repeating the clues aloud, she called out to Simon.

"I think it's a book mark. I mean, think about it. A page can be found when I am the guide. What else can it be?" and both began the search for any book containing a bookmark.

Jade stopped, she could hear the distant voice of her uncle scream with delight.

"Whoo hoo! I found it, I found it."
Simon cheered, a small section of the puzzle piece was jutting out of a novel. He looked down to his niece.

"You know, squirt, we make a good team."
Simon reached for the book, ceasing as he studied the spine. It read, 'What goes up, must come down'. The warning was obvious.

"Hey, squirt," he called to Jade again. She answered, acknowledging that she could hear. "I want you to climb down to your mother before I take this book out, okay. And no arguments."

He watched as his niece descended the fifty odd shelves that she had climbed. Pickwick scurried to her chest pocket and snuggled in safely.

"Okay, I'm down, now," but Simon could not hear, however, he did see her.

Therese opened the gateway, forcing her children through.

"Please, mum, I want to watch," Jade begged, disappointed when her mother disagreed, asking her to close the door and watch her brother.

Simon watched from above, waiting for the okay from Therese, she waved and gave the thumbs up, informing him the children were safe.

"Here goes," Simon took hold of the book, and opened it.

Nothing happened.

The puzzle piece sat between two pages, smaller than the others they had obtained. Simon grasped the piece and began to descend when suddenly there was movement. The bookshelf began to sway, and the books began to vibrate. Within seconds, thousands of paperbacks and hard cover publications shot out from the pockets where they rested, ready to pelt down.

"Go in," he yelled to his sister over the noise of crashing books. "The books are coming down and the shelf will crush you."

Therese hesitated for a moment but hearing the muffled voice of her brother pleading, she granted his wish, closing the door behind her.

Simon hurried his descent as books rained down, shooting characters and objects in every direction. He could feel the puzzle piece expand in his grip. Managing to maneuver it, he secured it under his arm. This slowed the climb with only one arm free and, to make matters worse, his balance destabilized as pelting books hit his torso. Unable to hold on any longer, he felt himself fall in slow motion, more books rained on him and the shelf began creaking forward.

He hit the surface, with a thump, covered in a blanket of books as more struck him with force.

Therese stood by the door with her ear against it, listening when she heard the wail of her brother falling towards the gateway. Now hearing the thud, she threw open the door and dragged Simon through in a panic, tears streaming down her face. She slammed the gateway shut. Jade ran toward the doorway and looked in horror when she saw her mother cry, leaning over her limp uncle.

"Nooo! Please," screamed Therese, shaking her brother and attempting to awaken him from the limp state.

Jade kneeled beside her mother, preparing to cast her healing power, still shaking when Simon stirred, elbowing himself to a seated position.

"Boy, did that knock me for a six," he rubbed his head tenderly. "Jeepers I'm glad I put the cuff near my head, or I probably would've had some real damage."

Therese and Jade sighed with a shaken relief, tears still cornered their eyes. Topaz had entered earlier and watched the devastation in action she too had watery eyes.

Other than a lot of bruising and stings of paper cuts, Simon was well enough to stand and take the puzzle piece to its place. The piece fused with the others leaving one completed row and two more pieces to go; they were close to the end and closer to finding Medwin.

"Hey, squirt," Simon forced a smile, "what do you say to another dose of your power. I'm getting used to it, annnd I think, I just might have a couple of fractures."

Jade responded immediately her concern apparent, watching as the bruising and paper-thin cuts faded. Micky fluttered above his uncle, his face crossed with a frown and his index finger pointed, shaking at his uncle.

"Yu no shleep, ucle shimod, okaiy. Shee mama cwy," he squealed, and berated his uncle, thinking his mother cried because Simon was asleep.

Pickwick stood on the puzzle board tapping his foot in deep thought. "Now Pickwick see, me do. You is sad when somebody's is hurt. Pickwick not make you sad, never again, I sorries. Pickwick will makes you's happy now, cause I loving me Jade family, I do's."

Pickwick finally realised why the family were upset when they thought he had drowned. The family took turns giving Wicks a hug. Jade held him last, giving him a scratch on his head and he broke into his contagious fit of giggles, causing the family to join in, laughing away the horror of the last gateway.

Topaz led the family to the kitchen, offering each member a glass of mulberry wine before retreating to the next gateway. "I brewed it myself," she said, "made only from the freshest berries I..."

Therese, Jade, and Simon interrupted, all finishing the sentence for her, "picked them myself from the orchard. We know!"

Topaz laughed with the family, mockingly dropping her lip. "Am I really that predictable? Oh, you lot. Come along, drink up! Gateway eight awaits."

Topaz and the family had grown fond of each other; Therese had also come to enjoy the possums cooking abilities.

"Yum!" Therese said but she was worried, "do you really think the kids should be drinking it? I don't think they should have wine."

Topaz assured her it was fine, adding that the brew had not fermented; therefore, it was not going to affect the children at all. The family quenched their thirst and emptied the jug of mulberry wine, ready for the next adventure. Jade led the way again as they approached an orange door, eager for an answer.

Chapter 21

WHATEVER YOU SAY

"I'm waiting, well come on, what do you say," it asked with wide eyes. "I'm waiting."

Simon leaned forward, turning the knob.

"Okay, okay," he said to the impatient door and revealed the gateway.

They entered the world, finding only a blank white canvas, including the ground they stood on.

"This is not cool," complained Jade, looking about seeing stark white in every direction. "Why can't it be like candy land or any other place would be better."

Therese agreed. "If only there was someone to meet us, so we know whcre to go. It all looks the same. Where do we start?"

Simon scanned the sterile area, searching for anything that may give them some indication.

"There's nothing," he said. "We need a sign, or something."

Signs began to appear everywhere, some on pickets, others suspended in air containing road safety symbols, symbols for ladies' and men's room, arrows, written signs with exit, entry, U-turn, koala crossing, neighborhood watch, wrong way, secretary, teller, do not disturb. There were hundreds, all with a unique message, adding confusion for the family and still they were unable to determine what direction to take.

"Great!" Therese complained now, "this world is really stupid, what do we do now?" she asked Simon as he searched the surroundings further.

"There should be a path; all the others had something like that," Simon grunted still searching.

Suddenly a reel of red carpet rolled itself up to where they stood.

"Cool," Jade said. "At least we know where to start, but I wish there was some candy or fun things at least."

They stepped on the carpet and began their walk.

Simon studied the signs along the path and read each one aloud, he began to feel irritated "these signs don't help; if anything, they're more confusing. I wish they weren't here."

Clouds of puffs appeared, raining down hundreds of little Pickwicks, looking very much like Wicks only they had different coloured arms, legs, and eyes. Wicks squeaked with excitement, waving to his friends as they scurried about removing the picketed signs. Groups jumped on each other's shoulders, creating towers, reaching high to collect the suspended ones. Within seconds all the signs were carried off, disappearing with the Pickwicks.

"What just happened?" Therese asked, with an idea creeping up within her mind. "Everything seems to happen when you say it, Simon."

She was right. They had entered the world of Simon Says. Nudging Simon, she prompted him to ask for something else. He was quick to respond.

"I'd love a mountain of hamburgers and fries. Big, thick, chocolate shakes would be good too and don't forget the straws."

Then multiples of burgers and chips dropped from the open sky, forming mounds in every direction. Giant thick shake containers fell with a thud, followed by curled straws that bent any which way.

"Wow," exclaimed Jade. "Ask for more, like chocolate bars and ice cream."

Simon followed her request, both laughing as stacks of chocolate and scattered bowls, full of ice cream scoops appeared. Simon began an obsession with his grants, asking for a lounge chair and TV sets, showing football games. Better still, he thought, *I want the footy played live, with a rock band playing their motto.*

Lounge room furniture and televisions popped out from the surface and fields morphed, dropping football players within as they proceeded to play the game with bands standing on stages, singing football chants. Simon was ecstatic, even his thoughts worked, this gateway was definitely his favourite then a smile cornered his lips.

"Hands on your heads," Simon said.

The family felt a force push their palms on top of their heads, excluding Simon. Therese leered at him and he quickly reversed the situation, still laughing, at least he thought it was funny. His mind was filling with desires and he continued asking for things.

"I'd like a solar powered Ferrari, Lamborghini, a Jacuzzi, and some gorgeous maids cooking, lots of pasta and..."

"Macaroni cheese and noodles too." Jade called out.

Simon repeated the words, now surrounded by clutters of his requests. Therese stood staring at the two as she pulled Micky out of an ice cream bowl. Pickwick scurried over, frantically wiping his sloppy face and hands.

"Enough you two!" hollered Therese. "We'll be squashed if you keep going. Simon please, clear some of this mess and ask for the puzzle piece."

Simon took hold of his obsession, shaking his head. "I'm so sorry, I don't know what came over me. I just got too excited, I guess," he then asked for the path to clear. "It was pretty cool though. But your right, I'll ask for the piece but let's get next to the exit first."
Jade was disappointed, still wanting to stay and have more fun with her uncle, complaining as she followed her mother.

The gateway was within reach. Everyone stopped, they were ready to enter and ready for the puzzle piece.

"Just one more thing," Simon pleaded with his sister, ready to say the words.

Therese laughed at his mania and rolled her eyes, they waited.

"Thanks sis. Now, I'd like a black Harley for me, a camo one for Jade, a red one for my sister," he grinned at Therese, "and a little one for Wicks, and a toy one for Micky."

Five motorbikes roared up, parking beside each owner. Jade cheered and hopped onto hers, it was perfect in height.

"I just thought some souvenirs would come in handy, eh," Simon smiled.

They all mounted their rides with Micky cushioned in front of his mother. Simon exhaled a deep breath, checking to see if everyone was ready and the bikes were in gear.

"I would like the puzzle piece in my hand, please," Simon said.

The piece appeared, Jade opened the door, and they all rode in, Simon followed last, feeling the rumble beneath his feet, he skidded his bike into a spin and closed the gateway.

"Yee ha! This is pretty cool, bro, great idea," bellowed Therese as their bikes roared to the puzzle board.

Simon hopped off his Harley, leaving it to idle and rushed to lay the piece in place, he was too excited about his bike and wanted to cruise more. He rushed back and mounted his bike once again then they rode about the house, with Pickwick following slowly behind. Everyone was laughing, the bikes were loud, and the house was large giving the family room to zoom about and race each other. Suddenly, they could feel the bikes soften as the metal began turning to ash. All five dissolved and faded until they were gone.

Topaz entered the room, looking at the somber faces.

"They were a creation from your imagination, Simon," she rattled. "They could not stay intact because they were not a solid form to begin with. Medwin, on the other hand placed the puzzle pieces in the gateway; therefore, they do not dissolve, because it was a solid form when it entered. I do hope you all cheer up; after all, there is only one more piece left to be retrieved."

The family looked at each other, smiling at the fur balls attempt to make them happy. They did have a wonderful time, particularly Simon and Jade, and after all, they did get to ride the bikes for some time. That was better than nothing.

No time to waste, they were all excited to be in position to retrieve the last puzzle piece, so they headed for the final gateway. Jade led them straight to the doorway, popping with joy. The end of the journey was close. They could find Medwin and open some of her favourite gateways again and she could not wait.

"Yuk," exclaimed Therese as they neared the entry.

It was a dusty mustard colour, unlike the other bright doors.

"Why do thy mock me, maiden," the door asked in a proper English voice.

"I'm sorry," replied Therese, "I suffer from foot in mouth disease sometimes. I was just expecting another bright colour, that's all. I really am sorry."

The door smiled, at least they thought it did, because its cheeks puffed slightly but its mouth was covered in long strands of facial hair.

"I most humbly forgive thee," it replied. "Enter thy gateway and behold the world of wonders."

Chapter 22

HISTORY EXPOSED

Simon entered, followed by the family and looked at the path they stood on. It was a long pinewood plank, ending through a shaft, surrounded by more timber. They began the trek forward cautiously and climbed through the narrow opening.

"Oh, no!" yelped Simon, jitters taking hold of his hands when a brute of a man snared him in a tight grip, as more men captured the remaining family.

The men wore woolen outer garments, layered with homespun, shaggy cloaks. On their feet were goatskin puttees, like sandals, followed by leg wrappings. Their heads were encased with tightly fitted helmets, made of leather and metal, some with a piece that extended down the nose.

"Super, cool bananas," Jade screeched, her adventure was just beginning. "We're on a Viking ship."

The path was in fact the oar of the Viking ship, leading through the pierced gun wall, but her excitement was settled somewhat when the family realised they were unwelcome guests on the ancient ship. The Viking oarsmen were startled at the intruders and reacted with force. Braced by two men each now, they were led from the galley, whilst the remaining men leered with eyes of anger.

Jade's fear was muffled by her excitement as she viewed and gasped at the internal surroundings of the ship. *This is unreal. I get to see history in real life*, she thought as they passed rows of woven baskets stored with beans, cereal stocks, wild fruit, and an assortment of herbs. Hanging off the rafters were sacks of animal skins stored with liquids and some simply drying, still wet with blood. Other liquids were contained within kegs stacked as high as the ceiling. The best, Jade thought, was a sector of wall adorned with long handled battle-axes, bronze and copper swords with twisted wire for handgrips, and tall silver spears.

Micky fluttered as two men struggled to grip his jiggling legs, giggling as he held his nose, "poo melly," he said, the stench of sweat and unwashed clothes filled the air with a sour smell.

Simon and Therese stared in awe when they caught sight of the twenty odd chests full of silver and gold bullion, making the suspicious barbarians poke their backs with the tips of their swords. They were led to a ladder, once again forced with a poke as they began ascending to the open air of the deck.

They now stood on the deck of a magnificent ship, stretching eighty feet in length, with curved prows at each end, carved into shapes of serpent heads, and centered was a single square sail, made of woven wool, with pale brown and plum stripes, that forced against the wind. The family watched with interest as the scene before them depicted more of the Viking heritage. Jade was trying to calm her excitement. This was fantastic. They were part of history. They could talk to the Vikings. They could see what they ate and did, but best of all they were standing on a Viking Long-ship, Whoo hoo!

The family braced themselves as they were led to the hull of the warship. More barbarians ogled at them, with war like intent, holding wooden shields, wearing similar clothes to the men below, but some wore goggle-like helmets. Some kneeled on the deck, glared briefly then continued playing their game, on a square wooden surface, tossing dice made of bones. Others sparred with spears and axes, whilst some wrestled with grunts from the sidelines. A group stood in a row tossing animal skins as judges stood at the opposite end, estimating their shot putt throws and drank from horned cups.

Simon's fear began to escalate as they approached the hull. "Please let us go, we come in peace," he pleaded. "We didn't know the gateway would bring us onto your ship. Please, please don't hurt the kids and my sister."

Standing at the hull was a tall aggressive figure, cursing at the approaching family surrounded by a group of barbarians that supervised iron cauldrons filled with carcasses of cattle and hogs. He was the ship captain, wearing a horned metal helmet that encased his disfigured face, his torso layered with animal skins, overlapped with a mesh vest.

"Why do thee barge, the voyage of the Norse serpent," he bellowed in a guff voice. "We do not endear to intruders." He pointed to the ship ledge and ordered, "Cast them overboard and allow the creatures of the sea to have with them, a feast."

The orders were acted on quickly and the family felt themselves fall to the awaiting diners.

Crack! "What, no splash!" Simon and the others opened their eyes.

They landed on a canoe filled with a tribe of men wearing splays of a feathered headdress and golden masks. Their necks and shoulders were tethered in ornate golden necklaces, which matched the cuffs secured to their wrists. Their chests were bare as were their feet. The only piece of clothing they wore was a skirt wrap, with detailed embroidery of ancient writings.

"Wow," Therese said, "I think these blokes are Aztecs."

Jade, overly excited now, agreed with her mother, both stopping in shock as the masked men stood up screaming at them in the ancient language.

There were flotillas of canoes filled with more Aztecs, all armed with spears, preparing for battle against the Vikings. Simon opened his mouth in an attempt to calm the tribe that began clutching them, but it was too late. The family felt themselves hoisted over the edge and tossed into the sea.

They floated, feeling uneasy, knowing that any minute now a passing sea creature could snap them. Suddenly, the feeling was escalated when they all felt a tongue like whip wrap itself around their bodies, forcing them below the water.

What the heck is that? Therese and the others thought. They struggled to free themselves from the metal ropes that were towed by a self-steered chariot. The ropes pulled the family to an awaiting glass cage, forcing them inside. A door appeared, creating a water tight seal, they were trapped.

"Mum... what's going on? I'm scared." Jade shivered.

Her mother aided with comfort, embracing a giggling Micky as well, not much bothered him. Pickwick scurried to Jades pocket and hid inside, he too was shivering.

"I don't know," Therese said. "Let's just see where it takes us and stay close, okay?" Therese continued a tight embrace and hummed to her children to calm the atmosphere. Simon stared, a feeling of hopelessness overcame him. He tried to break the glass but with no success.

Jade broke from her embrace. Jumping up, she pushed her face against the glass, staring as they approached their destination. It was a city with a central island fort surrounded by two rings of land. The last ring was edged with a stone fortress wall.

They entered the tall solid gold gates with carvings depicting notable events, people, and creatures and they all watched with open mouths, particularly Jade who tried to speak, but her excitement only made her gurgle.

The chariot towed the glass cage into the fort, planting it on the stone dock. The sealed door disappeared, and the whips reappeared, entangling each member once again and pulled them out. The whips stretched and carried the family towards some steps that ascended to the central city. The ropes placed them down and began winding back into the chariot.

They huddled together and climbed up the wide stairway, surprised that the ocean waters did not flood the city and most importantly, they were able to breathe. The ocean waters finished in a mist across the entire city in an octagonal dome.

"Wow!" exclaimed Jade. "What if it's Atlantis?"

"Ah," said an approaching man "I see we have an avid historian in our city."

The family looked as the man continued speaking in an indo-euro voice.

"I am Muvanos and you are most humbly welcomed to the city of Galina, calm of the sea. It brings me no pleasure to disappoint you young child." He looked at Jade. "We are descendants of Hittite not Atlantians; however, as the city of Atlantis, we too suffered the ferocious sea, and our land was swallowed by the waters." He pointed to a series of mounds in the near distance.

"They're underwater volcanoes," Jade gasped. "Gosh! You were pulled into the sea by a Tsunami."

Muvanos studied Jade for a moment, "I know not of what you speak. It was the wrath wave of Poseidon that delved our lands to the deep, and with stars guiding us, our leader, expediently enchanted our city to continue our way of life beneath the surface, you see. That is why the waters of the sea, cannot pass the mist."

The man led the family forward as they viewed magnificent domed temples including official abodes and local homes edged along canals leading to a ring of water. Lineages of pillars spread throughout, some were signs showing maps of the city, and others as tall statues, all carved of stone. Gardens of vineyards and olive groves covered vacant grounds, some temples with grape vines growing up the walls.

The people were a mixture of fair skinned and olive skin, all with dark hair. They wore soft, tall wizard hats, with tan cloaks floating above gold sandals, enclosed with upturned, pointed toes. Some carried storage vessels, the same pottery was placed about the pathways along with carved tablets. The family was in awe as they moved about the stone pathways, greeting the dwellers and gaining insight to their way of life.

Muvanos invited the family to feast on a communal table. The locals greeted and welcomed them, sharing stories as they sat on woven carpets made of dried ocean plants. Pottery filled with produce, wheat products and sea fruit were passed across the table as all feasted, followed by golden goblets containing grape cider. Therese and Simon enjoyed the food and the exchange of information between centuries. Jade glowed as she researched more of the Hittite Empire, even asking for any information they might have about Atlantis. Micky and Pickwick played with the younger locals, scurrying and fluttering about the place including knocking bowls and food onto the diners, when they played chase on the communal table.

The feast continued with merriment, when suddenly they felt a rumble below their feet.

"Do not be concerned," Muvanos said, "we often feel the shake on the ground; Poseidon wishes to keep us aware of his presence."

Simon watched the tremor on the surface, with a shadow of concern falling on his face. "The volcano is still active," he whispered to Therese. The tremor began to shake with more force. Simon gripped Micky and Pickwick as Therese embraced Jade. "Run!" he shouted. "It's about to blow."

Therese stared at her brother. "Where!" she shouted above the rumble. "Muvanos is there a safe place?" She spun as she asked the man, realising with fear that all the locals had disappeared leaving the family alone to deal with the eruption.

The stone slabs beneath their feet began to crack and spread to large gaps. Simon grasped hold of Therese and Jade still holding Micky and Pickwick as the current of water began to churn.

"Whatever happens just hold on, don't let go of each other," he yelled.

Then with intense force they felt the wave of water push them with immense speed toward the surface of the sea, propelling them farther toward the sands of an island. Simon pushed the family against a wide tree trunk, forcing his body against the family whilst he embraced the trunk with all his might. The wave of water began to pull back towards the open sea and the family felt the force trying to drag them back in, but with luck and Simon's strength they were able to remain attached to the tree.

Safe for now, Simon released his grip and they all fell backwards, onto the sand in exhaustion. Checking to see if everyone was okay, Simon and Therese began to stand, when arms reached down to aid them in their struggle. Unable to find the words, they stared at these things. Beasts, with the body of a human and the head of a Doberman.

Therese shook her head, "thanks for the boost, but who are you. Where are we?"

The creatures were silent; they bowed and pointed, directing the family down a path, separated by thick growths of palms and marshy growths. Simon led the way behind one of the creatures who guided them, Therese and Jade followed as Micky leapt on the canine creature for a piggyback, patting him on the head saying, "goo goggy."

The guide halted, gesturing Simon to step back from the tall growth of palms blocking the path. He then spoke the words, 'Pato Ed Medis', causing the block to shrink back to a form of seedlings, revealing a city of enormous triangular structures, masses of temples and sky scraper statues, surrounded by a river, edged with boat pits.

"Oh! My! Gosh!" Jades heart was beating fast. "It's ancient Egypt! Far out. This gateway is the coolest, it's the best. That's why that door said, 'world of wonders', history makes people wonder."

Jade could hardly control her excitement. Simon and Therese were not much better. They all shook with eagerness watching as they were led to the largest temple, held up by massive columns carved with hieroglyphics.

There was much commotion about, with more canine people constructing pyramids and others tending to wheat fields. There was a group acting a pantomime of a battle, whilst females danced about in dreamy sequence. Therese, Jade and Simon panicked when they spotted palm sized scarabs, scurrying about the place amongst the civilization, this did not seem to faze any of the inhabitants though.

They were directed to a stairway and began ascending towards the temple that sat high above the others it was to be a long climb. Suddenly the family felt the steps move beneath them. A giant asp appeared, becoming the surface on which they stood and slithered up toward the entry of the temple. This was much quicker.

A man sat on a throne, waiting, and placed his arms across his chest. His eyes glowed a yellow flame, instantly dissolving the asp the family rode upon. There were many forms of creatures attending to his needs including two pale blue, pygmy hippos, resting beside him and basking in the caress of their master.

"Greetings," the man said in a strong, almost cat-like voice. "I am Pharaoh. Do you have news of Topaz?"

The family looked at each other.

"You know Topaz?" asked Simon. "She's fine. In fact, she loves her life. She just misses Medwin."

"I am pleased by your answer." The Pharaoh turned his attention to Jade. "I can see your thoughts child, so I shall enlighten you. We are one with all animals. Observe."

He ordered a servant to transform. They stood open mouthed staring at the servant removing the face of the feline as it morphed into a human face and the other head formed into a Siamese cat.

"Wow," Jade gasped. "That was super cool and how did you know I was thinking that! That's freaky."

"Our culture understands energy. We have the ability to manifest all with this knowledge." The Pharaoh changed the subject. "You have trekked off your intended path." He then waved his hand in the direction of a light well as his eyes glowed once again. The cavity began to glow, shooting a beam of light to the floor. "Enter," he ordered. "This shall lead to your destination."

The Pharaohs servants edged the family to the ray and the suction pulled them through the light well. "Noooo," echoed Jade's voice; she wanted to stay and learn more about the Egyptian mysteries.

The ray vanished, and the family slid on the cushioned grass of a field. It looked quite normal, Simon thought until his sisters' scream alerted him to attention.

"Move everyone and jump for cover!" Therese shouted.

A large kite flew towards them, nearly hitting them had they not moved in haste. "What now?" yelped Simon as a puff of dirt filled the air.

A disorientated man stepped out of the crash, wobbling over to the family as another ran toward them, cheering for the previous flight.

"Are you hurt?" he asked. "I do so apologise. These test flights are becoming successful; however, the landing did not go well, and I was startled when I saw you all in the path. You must be the family Medwin advised of. It is quite an honour to meet you all. My name is Wilbur; the fellow running towards us is Orville, my brother and co-inventor."

This time it was Simon's turn to be excited; they were the Wright brothers, the inventors of flight. This was fantastic. They had lived in the early 1900's and Simon had done a project about them in high school.

The brothers led the family back to their home to prepare the glider needed for the flight back. On reaching the house, they showed the family directly to their next way of travel. Simon became nervous and adamant he could not do it

"What!" Simon was surprised "What do you mean, we will be doing it. I've never had to fly a plane before, how the heck am I supposed to fly this one?"

"I'll have a go," Therese said. "There's always a first time for everything, ha," she smiled, attempting to hide the butterflies fluttering in her stomach.

Orville briefed Therese on flying the contraption as the others were strapped tightly to the wings. The brothers then rapidly constructed a temporary rail to act as a runway. Therese stood before the glider with a gas-powered engine and two propellers, building up the courage needed for her first flight as a pilot.

"You shall be fine," Wilbur said. "We studied birds in flight to enable us to construct this wonderful plane. Now, listen carefully, there is a cloud above the Viking long-ship. You must land the glider upon this cloud. The puzzle piece rests within the surface, and further, you must reenter the ship to retrieve a silver bullion from the Viking chest. Medwin was adamant that you will need it to complete the puzzle board."

Therese was propped into the glider and began to power the engine. Off they went as the Wright brothers waved, watching the plane lift at the fourth rail, they were airborne.

'Whoo hoo!" Simon and Jade cheered, firstly for Therese and secondly because it was quite fun.
Therese gripped the rudder, trying to keep the rise and avoid the plane from darting to the surface below. The plane pitched with jerks until she felt confident and was able to settle in to a smooth flight. She smiled widely when she heard Simon bellow.

"You're a natural, sis," he shouted, the wind pelting against his face.

"Go Ma!" Jade and Micky called out.

It was quite serene. They passed through clouds, looked at the views below seeing lands they had visited, during their trek in the gateway.

"There it is, mum," Jade yelled, pointing in the direction of the Viking ship.

Therese scanned for the cloud. Spotting it instantly, she headed for the landing.

"Not bad," Simon was impressed. The landing had minor vibrations, but it mostly went smoothly.

"I'm getting a pilot license when we find Medwin. That was unreal. Now, let's get the kids back through the gateway to safety first, then we'll deal with the puzzle piece." Therese pulled the folded cushion from her pocket and thought for a moment.

"Ask for an elastic potion, mum. Then we can stretch to the oars," Jade said.

Therese wasted no time, she pulled out a mug filled with lime green slush. They all took part in drinking, except for Micky, Therese wanted to hold him, to avoid any cheeky actions. Pickwick was fine too, he was tucked into Jade's pocket the button threaded for extra safety.

"Cool, watch this everyone." Jade stretched her arms and holding both hands together; she created a silhouette of a large heart within the gap.

Therese and Jade sat on the edge of the cloud stretching their legs until their feet touched the surface of the oar, leading to the gateway. Then slowly with Micky and Pickwick secured, they descended, reducing their legs to their original states. Simon agreed to stay put on the cloud and await the consent from Therese before retrieving the puzzle piece.

"That was fun, weird but fun," Jade stated, then began a plea with her mother to stay just outside of the exit.

Therese agreed, asking that she wrap an arm around Micky, but as soon as she returned from the ship, they were to enter before Simon took hold of the puzzle piece. Jade was happy with the compromise, wrapping two arms around her brother, assuring there was no way of escape and she watched her mother approach the pierced gun walls of the ship.

Therese focused and studied the surface of the timber then camouflaging herself with the structures, she was ready. All was going well as she entered, stretching her arms and swinging off the rafters, like monkey bars, still made of wood.

She now hung above the chests full of bullions. Thinking for a moment, Therese studied the surfaces below, noting that her arm would need to blend with the surfaces as it stretched down. *Boy! This is overload on texture studies*, she thought. Inhaling a deep breath, she extended her arm and gripped a silver bullion then began to swing rapidly back to the exit, not realising the bullion was not camouflaged. The Vikings began a rampage, bellowing that evil was aboard, scurrying and stomping their way out, up the ladder.

Therese climbed back through the cavity. "I got it, quick get your piece," she yelled to Simon and then called out to Jade, "quick, go inside. They've spotted your uncle."

The Vikings that scurried above to the deck were bellowing about the evil spirits as others looked above spying Simon on the cloud. They began tossing their spears and battle axes, managing to gain hits against the glider.

"Hurry," yelled Therese, her nerves were a mess.

Simon stretched his legs down to the oar. Then twisting, he grabbed the puzzle piece and began to descend. "I've got it. Run inside. I'm almost there."

Simon slowly lowered himself down to the oar, dodging the battle weapons in flight. "Ouch," he yelped, as a spear sliced the edge of his arm, seconds before his body returned to its original state. Beginning his sprint, he felt the oars dropping below his feet the long-ship was sinking. He reached for the knob and tossed himself through the doorway. "Phew," he gasped, slowly calming his breath, watching the ship bubble into the waters below as he closed the gateway.

"Well, well, well, the avid adventurers have returned." Topaz entered the room, feeling the impact of Micky, she nearly toppled over from the hug. "Oh, thank you, Micky. I do love the hugs, perhaps a little gentler next time, hm?" They both giggled.

"Come on, let's get this last piece in place. I can't wait to see what happens," Simon said and waited for Therese to grip Micky.

They began the walk towards the dining area and as they approach the game board, their anticipation grew. During the walk, without taking a breath, Jade shared the details of their last experience with Topaz and how the Pharaoh was pleased to hear of the possum.

"I didn't think possums lived in Ancient Egypt," she drew back a gulp of oxygen. She was quite surprised to learn that Topaz had come from that particular gateway. She wanted to know more, there was so much still left to mystery. "Oh no! Uncle Simon," she was distracted when she saw the blood trickling down his arm, her uncle was hurt.

"Don't worry, the wound can wait, it's really not that bad," Simon stated and passed the puzzle piece to Jade, "there you go squirt, you can have the honours."

With more excitement Jade grasped the piece and began to lay it in place slowly, she wanted to prolong the suspense.
Suddenly, the board shuddered. Jades face paled.

"Nooo!" she bellowed, her excitement crushed. "It's growing."

This cannot be happening; there are no more doors left!

The puzzle board doubled in size adding a further eight pieces with a centered message aglow spelling HEIST.

MEDWIN'S ROOM

BOOK 2

"No…..no, no, no. This isn't fair," hollered Jade with apparent anger in her voice. "What now! Heist, what's that mean?"

The family stood in despair, joined by Topaz the brush-tailed possum. This cannot be, not even Topaz had foreseen this. Medwin had been thorough with the bewitchment he had left for the chosen ones to follow. Were the obstacles the family had experienced not enough? Obviously not!

There was a sudden thump. Jade, Micky, and Simon jumped at the sound and turned to the sight. Therese had collapsed at what Simon thought was an overwhelming disappointment because the puzzle board had expanded. However, this was not the case; blue smoke began to float off her body like dry ice and coiled as it met above her unconscious body.

"Muuum!" Jade screeched, and her baby brother Micky began to cry.

They all ran to Therese's side. Simon reached over but was unable to touch his sister. The smoke created a solid barrier stopping any physical contact.

They could only watch in horror not knowing what was happening or what was to come.

The smoke continued to billow into a coil and began to change to a vivid purple. Then suddenly, the coil released and shattered into tiny specks burying Therese in a mound of sand. The family just stood in shock, unable to move, afraid that she was dead, but to great relief they saw movement. Therese stood up and with multiple swoops, she dusted off the remaining residue.

Topaz rushed by her side, rattling with concern. Never had she seen magic in this context. Medwin had taught this possum quite a lot. It was the purple smoke, as bright as a neon light, which concerned her the most. What could it mean?

The possum clawed off in haste her brush tail spiked with fright, dread gripping her thoughts. Could Therese have contracted sorcery within the gateways? She sped towards the den; she needed to enter the canvas to find some answers in Medwin's library.

Topaz climbed through the frame and entered the enormous domed library, towering twenty-seven stories high with walls leaning on angles, as though on the verge of collapse. Within these walls were thousands of scattered niches, housing dusty books and scrolls, some leather bound, some appearing like stone tablets.

"Follington," hollered Topaz, panic still apparent in her voice. "Follington, quickly find me all that can be known on neon purple smoke—and hurry."

Follington zoomed up the spiral of the levitating books centered in the library. His hover ski attached to his suede foot screamed towards the enormous glass dome. He reached into his pouch and pulled out a small clump of coal then tossed it at the glass. Suddenly, the glass evaporated revealing the night sky with constellations of stars pushing themselves forward to reveal symbols. Follington forced his telepathy until he felt all symbols needed revealed the whereabouts of this information. Then extracting a fireball from within his pouch again, he tossed it towards the dome transforming it back to daylight.

Topaz watched with impatient jerks and deep rattling breaths. *That Follington is a gem,* she thought. In fact, his skin shimmered like a jade stone and his humanlike body differed from a face sharpened in a lion-like snout, with large black feline eyes that watered with intensity. His precious knowledge and advanced technological skills were a blessing to Medwin, Jupiter, or was it Exos; Topaz could never remember which galaxy this Alien was born.

In a fraction of a second, Follington removed the required tablet from within a niche and began running his twig-like hand across the clear glass, deciphering the vibrations as he approached the plump possum.

Topaz stood alert absorbing this information. "But this could only mean, oh dear."

The possum strained to hold her composure, her emotions and body on the verge of collapse in thought of her good friend and Master, Medwin.

About the Author

Termina Ashton, also known as 'The Happy Magnet', has the uncanny ability to tilt the odds so the best will happen. She resides with her family in Queensland, Australia where she lives a lifestyle of fun, joy and opportunities, and believes in navigating her own world of experiences through imagination, and Feng Shui. Termina, a mentor, author, illustrator, Feng Shui expert, and an interior designer has worked on many projects both residential and commercial including an open design radio station, Fox Studios and a variety of set designs where her own artwork was exhibited for TV and film.

Termina began writing novels to put down on paper the rampant images and adventures that filled her mind, and in doing so, has captured the imagination of children and adults all around the world. Termina is delighted her books have become so popular and is equally delighted when some describe her as Australia's answer to Enid Blyton. Termina believes a reason for the popularity is...

"No matter how old; we all like to escape into the world of imagination and creating my world is what I do, anything is possible, we should all endeavour to follow our passion, everyone has talents, push up your sleeves and take action. There is joy in doing what we love, and the results are always wonderful"

Festival of the Imagination is one of many non-fiction books by Termina. Termina calls herself a student of self-actualization. It was through her studies and introspection practices that she was able to tap into her unique soul signature and states that she is guided by source. *"At all times we carry with us all the answers. There is nothing in the physical world that will truly give us the ultimate answer; our unique soul print and purpose in life; and it is because of this only ourself has the true answers for what makes us happy or why we are here. We only require external tools, or mentors to get us started and guide us in a direction towards connecting with our soul's voice. With the right tools and mentors, we are on our way to unleashing our true, powerful self."*

Termina credits self-actualization practices for her success and harmony in her life. Another one she credits is Feng Shui as a guide to alignment for choices. *"It was through my studies and practice of Feng shui that I discovered the importance this ancient art plays in our life. 33% of our experiences are created through our physical visualization board, our environment. When we apply the principles of Feng Shui our lives become the choices we desire, we are in control of our own experiences at all times and good fortune is attainable. Through Feng Shui I have seen improvements and successes in my own life along with the many others who have appointed my services."*

For more information about this author
and other books:
www.terminaashton.com
www.perpelflame.com
www.terminafengshui.com
www.thehappymagnet.com

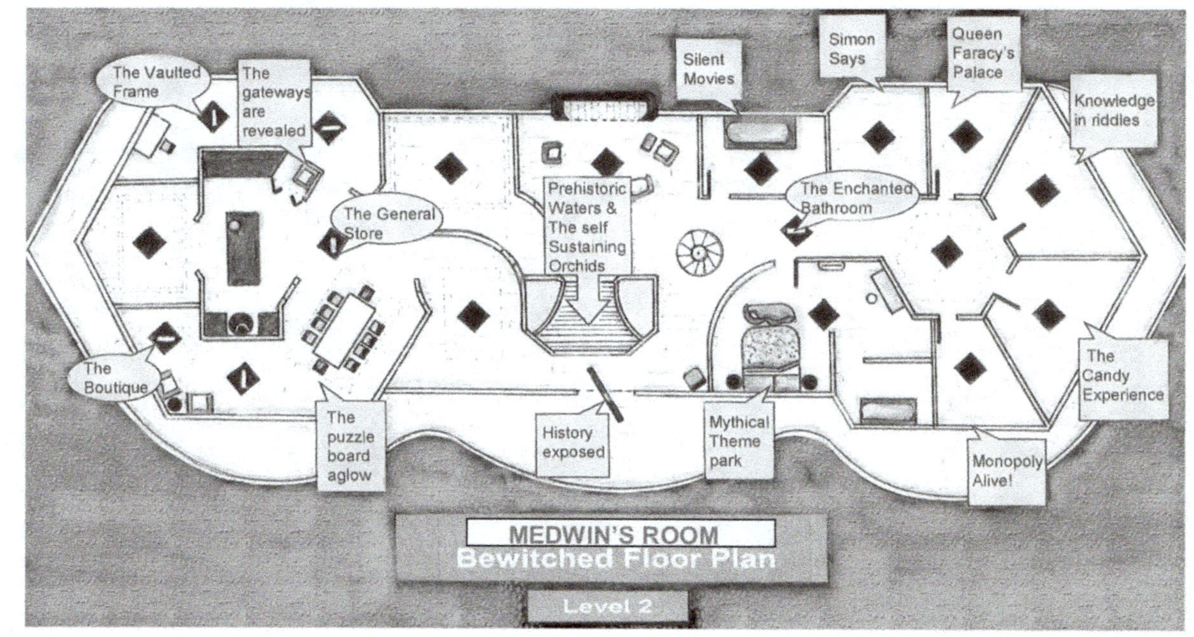
The Vaulted Frame
The gateways are revealed
Silent Movies
Simon Says
Queen Faracy's Palace
Knowledge in riddles
Prehistoric Waters & The self Sustaining Orchids
The General Store
The Enchanted Bathroom
The Boutique
The puzzle board aglow
History exposed
Mythical Theme park
The Candy Experience
Monopoly Alive!
MEDWIN'S ROOM
Bewitched Floor Plan
Level 2